His change of mood made Catherine uneasy.

'And I suppose you think *you* can solve everything just like magic?' she challenged. 'Everyone will suddenly take up their beds and walk, leaving all the drip poles and trailing tubes?'

Matthew Dunnegan refused the bait and his lips began to curve into a teasing grin. 'Not exactly, no. But someone ought to take things in hand.'

Dear Reader

We travel again this month, to Spain and Australia in SWEET DECEIVER by Jenny Ashe, and OUTBACK DOCTOR by Elisabeth Scott. We also welcome back Elizabeth Fulton with CROSSMATCHED where American new broom Matt Dunnegan shakes up renal nurse Catherine, and Mary Bowring, who returns with more of her lovely vet stories in VETS IN OPPOSITION. Just the thing to curl up with by the fire as winter nights draw in! Enjoy.

The Editor

Recent titles by the same author:

DELICATE HARMONY
RESEARCH FOR LOVE

CROSSMATCHED

BY

ELIZABETH FULTON

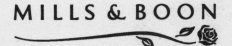

MILLS & BOON LIMITED
ETON HOUSE, 18–24 PARADISE ROAD
RICHMOND, SURREY, TW9 1SR

*First published in Great Britain 1993
by Mills & Boon Limited*

© Elizabeth Fulton 1993

*Australian copyright 1993
Philippine copyright 1993
This edition 1993*

ISBN 0 263 78376 6

*Set in 10 on 11 pt Linotron Times
03-9311-55437*

*Typeset in Great Britain by Centracet, Cambridge
Made and printed in Great Britain*

CHAPTER ONE

THE man's face was blurred, and Catherine Woodley squinted at the indistinct features less than an inch from her nose.

'I wish they'd stuck a mirror over the crack instead of a KPA bulletin.' She jabbed a pin into the starched cap threatening to slide off her upswept auburn curls. 'I'm tired of looking at the ugly blob every day for the past week.'

'Oh, I don't know about that. The new one looks a hunk.' The round face of her best friend edged closer to the notice taped on the staff room wall. 'He sure stands out. Absolutely towers over the professor!'

Catherine snorted, 'Even *I* tower over our dear old Prof. You ready, Em? Time to get on with our professional support of the Kidney Patients' Association and our current benefactors. This time it's a new Cobe machine, isn't it?'

Emily tossed her disposable apron into the bin and tightened her uniform belt before holding open the locker-room door. 'So Sister said, but where we're going to find the space for it is anybody's guess.' As she stood in the corridor she looked back. 'You haven't forgotten Josh's birthday this Sunday, have you?'

'Of course not!' The prospect of joining in a family party was part of Catherine's general feeling of contentment with the world. Everything was just as it should be, and she looked forward to the reaction to her carefully chosen gift.

Hurrying to follow her fellow staff nurse, Catherine dodged the tall machines lining the long corridor, from long habit expertly avoiding the crates of purified water and dialysate piled against the walls. Without pausing, she glanced into each of the three large rooms they passed.

Through the glass panels she could see that all the patients were resting comfortably as they began their long sessions of renal dialysis. She no longer noticed the background drone of humming and whirring that accompanied the treatments literally giving each patient a new lease of life.

At the edge of the crowded lecture-room, Catherine edged into an unobtrusive place near the door. Mrs Blessington was well launched into her effusive speech of gratitude to the donors of the gleaming new dialysis machine standing in the centre of the semi-circle of listeners.

All she could see of the president of the KPA was the bobbing of a large feathered hat, and she craned her neck, trying to spot the professor. Ah, there he was, standing with his head attentively cocked and his hands jammed into his coat pockets.

As a smattering of applause greeted the end of Mrs Blessington's words, Catherine tried to see the professor's face. He would speak next, and she liked to listen to his gentle cultivated voice. This was one of the rare occasions when he had visited the unit recently, and she frowned in irritation. Something or someone was blocking her view.

She shifted position to look over Emily's shoulder, and her breath caught in her throat. For a moment her eyes were dazzled by the unexpected sight.

Behind the professor stood a tall figure bathed in an opalescent glow. The brightness of the shimmering halo around the shadowed form hurt to look at, and Catherine blinked rapidly. She knew the image was an optical illusion, a trick of the morning sun reflected through a window, but the vision had an eerie and unlikely resemblance to a silver knight in shining armour.

She narrowed her eyes. That armour was just a brand-new medical coat fresh from the hospital laundry and probably with too much starch in it. So this must be the new transplant surgeon, replacing the surgical assistant who had so precipitately departed less than a month ago. She turned her attention to the professor, who had begun to introduce the newly arrived staff member.

'. . .are indeed honoured to have him, with his extensive experience in America. . .'

The subject of this speech shifted his weight uncomfortably. The hip pain was spreading and he kept his hands clenched behind his back. If he didn't get to sit down soon, he would fall down, and a fine introduction that would make! A quick movement by the door caught his eye as a shaft of autumn light flashed like a flame at the edge of his sight.

Now there was a fine figure of a woman! That hair in the sunlight was just the colour of leaves in a New England fall—rich red with hints of brown. Glorious. He wondered what colour her eyes were. Hazel, maybe with hints of something? Green or gold? Briefly a smile tugged at the edge of his mouth. The cap perched on top of that burnished head was cheerfully askew; he liked that touch. A neat figure in her tidy white uniform, but that cap! He wished she'd glance at him again, but her attention seemed riveted on the professor, worse luck.

'. . .following his latest work in paediatric renal transplants in Toronto. I hope you will all join with me in welcoming Matthew Dunnegan to the St Damien's team.'

A dutiful moment of handclapping ended his introduction, and the new doctor forced a smile as the unit sister approached to shake his hand. Matthew Dunnegan noted the quick exit of the girl with the crooked cap and resigned himself to the continued discomfort of fending off polite platitudes.

'Would you join us on a ward round, Matthew?' Professor Wilkins peered up at his new assistant. 'We have some very interesting problems here at the moment.'

'Delighted, sir.' Feeling a genuine sense of relief at the opportunity of physical movement, Matthew Dunnegan immediately divested himself of the thick china cup pushed at him by the smiling staff nurse at his side. 'Thanks very much. Must go, I'm afraid.'

'Pleasure, Mr Dunnegan.' Emily had taken the opportunity to get a closer look at this man, and she liked what she saw.

The undeniable warmth in her voice made him hesitate. 'Is that a tinge of Louisiana I hear? Don't tell me there's another Yank in these depths of suburban England?'

Emily smiled. 'Not me, Mr Dunnegan. I must have picked up the accent from my husband, Josh. He's from a place called Baton Rouge.' She noticed his nod of recognition. 'You have good ears.'

He grinned at her. 'Well. . .' looking down at her name tag '. . .Mrs E. Beatty, I'll probably get a fair earful from the professor if I don't follow him PDQ. Thanks again.'

'Any time, Mr Dunnegan.' Emily watched him walk slowly away before she moved to clear the tea trolley. She'd always had a fondness for Americans, and he was good-looking, with those grey eyes that had been watching them over by the door. She doubted it was herself who had been the focus of his attention, and she smiled thoughtfully.

Catherine had hurried away to check on all the patients who already knew the professor was visiting; a buzz of happy expectation had been added to the general ambience of relaxation. The women were straightening their nightgowns or ruffled hair, while the men put aside their newspapers and sat up, just in case they were to be examined by the one physician they all trusted with their lives.

'How does he look?' The loud whisper came from a middle-aged woman who had put aside her thick paper-backed novel.

Catherine answered absently, 'Just fine, Mrs Murphy.' Her gaze was fastened on the child in the next bed, lying with eyes closed and one arm curled around a large stuffed panda. There was a fine sheen of perspiration on the little girl's forehead, and Catherine adjusted the overhead fan to a higher level, carefully directing it away to one side. 'Has Jackie been asleep long?' she asked.

'Like a baby, for the last hour.' Mrs Murphy looked over. 'So pretty, she is! It's all right for the likes of me, all this palaver, but such a pity —— Oi, heads up! Here they come.'

Her warning brought Catherine's attention back to her duties. Hoping the child would be allowed to sleep, she moved to ready the patients' notes, not that the professor ever asked for them. He had supervised the treatment of the dialysis patients for the many years they had been attending.

As the small group moved slowly around the circle of patients, Catherine surreptitiously kept an eye on the newest addition. There was something about the white-coated figure that bothered her, but she couldn't put a finger on it. He appeared to be listening carefully as the professor exchanged pleasantries with each of the patients, but was saying nothing.

Not much of a bedside manner, she thought, as she kept each set of notes ready in turn. Now they were moving towards Jackie's bed, and she could see the tall man was moving strangely, almost dragging one foot. Some white knight! This Lancelot had a limp. And he was looking very severe, in contrast to the pleasant, gentle smile of the professor.

Now they were discussing the little girl, and Catherine edged closer. Jackie was special, and she wanted to hear what was being said.

'I'm sure this one will interest you, Matthew.'

'Indeed.' Matthew Dunnegan moved to the head of the child's bed and gazed at her without expression. He didn't like what he saw, but he would need to know more. If only his damn hip would ease up he might be able to think more clearly. Too many memories kept crowding in, and he shook his head quickly to brush away the cobwebs.

The gesture made Catherine frown. She knew how difficult the situation was for Jackie, but he didn't have to make a negative prognosis without even knowing her.

'A phone call, Professor.' Emily appeared at the edge of the group.

'Thank you. I'll leave you to it, then, Matthew.'

'Right.' Without moving, the surgeon remained standing at the bedside as the others drifted away in the wake of the departing professor.

He reached for the child's hand, and Catherine spoke without thinking.

'No, you'll wake her.'

'That's what I intend.' He spoke without turning, his eyes fastened on the flushed face against the pillow.

'Mmm?' The child mumbled, and turned her head. China-blue eyes opened wide at the sight of a stranger. 'Who're you?'

'My name is Matt.' His voice was deep and quiet, and Catherine was surprised at the warmth as well as the soft smile on his face. He really was quite handsome when he smiled, if you liked the rugged type.

She watched as the child examined her visitor carefully. 'You're not St Nick?' queried Jackie.

'Not that I know of. You were expecting someone else?'

Catherine tried to explain. 'She means——'

'I know who she means.' Again he spoke without taking his eyes away from the little girl. '"In hopes that St Nicholas soon would be there."' He took the small hand in his and turned it over with great care, gently pressing on each fingernail. 'Does this hurt?'

'Not really.' The blue eyes were struggling to open more widely. 'My name's Jackie.'

'Thank you, Miss Jacqueline.' An exaggerated drawl brought a tentative smile to the pale face, and he tucked her hand under the cotton sheet. He nodded to himself as he straightened slowly. 'I guess I'll have to have a word with St Nick about you.'

'Really?' The little girl snuggled back against her pillow. 'Do you think he'll bring me a new kidney?'

'You just keep on wishing, Miss Jackie. Sometimes wishes can come true, so you can't give up on them. You know that?'

'I know.' She was nearly back to sleep. 'Do you think you can help him find one for me?'

Matthew Dunnegan watched as the eyelids closed. 'I'll have to do my best to see that he finds just the right one, Miss Jackie.'

The child's words were barely audible. 'That's good.'

As he stood back from the bed, Matthew looked around and found the patient's chart being held out to him by the nurse with the shining auburn hair. He glanced at the top of her head and his lips twitched briefly. 'Ah, thank you.'

And just what did he find so humorous? Catherine kept her facial expression blank and her lips firmly shut. He had just woken up a sleeping patient who needed all the rest she could get, to talk about fantasies. Jackie's chances of getting a suitable transplant were minimal, and everyone here knew it. What made him think he could promise the impossible?

Now he was frowning at the notes in his hands, and Catherine could guess why. She decided to say nothing unless requested, as a proper subordinate, since he had already ignored her so effectively. Let him figure things out for himself, if he was so certain he knew everything.

They had moved away from the bed, and Matthew was leaning against the portable note rack. As he flicked through the clinical laboratory results Catherine wedged her foot under the nearest castor wheel. His considerable weight was threatening to send them skidding across the room, and she wondered if she should try and find this limping Lancelot a chair.

'Have the relatives been tissue-typed and crossmatched?'

His question sounded brusque, and Catherine answered, 'Yes, Doctor.'

'Parents?' His eyebrow lifted as he glanced at her. A bit tetchy, this one.

'Not suitable.'

'Does she have any siblings?' Maybe she was just being formal, but that bland tone sounded forced.

'One sister, aged four. Possibly compatible, but one kidney appears not to be growing.'

He nodded and sighed. Spare-part surgery was a misnomer. No one had any spare parts to give away lightly; everything had a purpose, even if no one yet knew all the interwoven functions for each organ in the human body. And this nurse was not being particularly helpful. He longed for a place to sit down.

'Thank you.' He glanced at her name tag and his face relaxed into a semblance of a smile. 'Miss C. C. Woodley.' That was an easy one to remember. He turned as if to make for the door and with a sudden lurch thudded against the sharp corner of the chart trolley.

His involuntary grunt of pain made Catherine wince. She had felt the jolt as if in her own bones, and she reached out to steady him.

''Ere then, Doctor, you mind where you're goin'!' Mrs Murphy had been eyeing the newcomer with interest.

'Sorry.' He blinked quickly. Really, this hip was being more trouble than he had expected. He shot a glare at the offending trolley and handed back Jackie's notes to the nurse looking at him with such obvious concern. She must think he was a suitable candidate for her professional ministrations. Not that that was such an unpleasant thought, but he made an effort to stand up straight.

'Well, then, you must be. . .'

As he paused, Catherine supplied the name he needed. 'Mrs Murphy is one of our oldest patients.'

'And that's the truth.' The woman's face was beaming. It was always a treat to see the young men who came to work with the professor, but this one looked especially nice, and handsome too. 'Don't you be botherin' yourself about me. Been 'ere an age, I have, and no mind to change things now.'

Matthew Dunnegan glanced at the tubes connected to the patient's arm, taking in the permanent fistula and the lower arms scarred from long usage for dialysis. He suspected her legs would have similar markings.

'It's rare to meet someone with no complaints,' he smiled.

'So long as my friend and me,' she patted the side of the thrumming machine beside the bed, 'get together, I'm all right. He keeps me goin', and if he keeps workin', then so do I.'

Knowing this patient was telling him she had no need or wish for his surgical services, Matthew nodded his understanding. The passivity of long-term dialysis patients was familiar, and he kept his disagreement with such an attitude to himself.

Mrs Murphy emphasised her point. 'So long as I'm doin' better than Phyllis there, I let things be.'

Puzzled, he rapidly reviewed the patients' names in his head. He couldn't remember a Phyllis anything, and he glanced at the nurse still standing at his elbow.

Catherine kept her face straight, enjoying just for a second the discomfiture on that angular face. The shadow of tension around the firm mouth made her relent. He really must still be in pain, and she spoke as if describing a clinical event.

'Phyllis,' she motioned with her hand, 'is a philodendron.'

'A. . .?'

'Been 'ere as long as I have, has Phyllis,' Mrs Murphy nodded firmly.

Both women watched as the doctor stared mutely at the straggling pot-plant nearly hidden in the folds of the flowered curtain covering the outside window. The heart-shaped leaves were drooping over the sill, winding themselves towards a spiny cactus.

Not knowing quite what he was expected to say about this occupant of the treatment-room, Matthew Dunnegan bit his lip thoughtfully. Using that wilted ivy thing as a criterion of good health was hardly an ambitious goal. Saying she felt better than that over-grown green tangle wasn't saying much.

'Looks to me as if you could both use a pick-me-up,' he remarked.

'Oh, we'll both survive for a bit yet, Doctor, don't you worry about that,' Mrs Murphy chortled. 'Been here for years, and we ain't finished yet.' She eyed him sharply. 'And don't you get any fancy ideas 'bout me, young man. Like things just the way they are, I do.'

He turned his glance to her and smiled. 'Message received and understood, Mrs Murphy. But your friend Phyllis might do well with some judicious pruning.'

'Jes' so long as you keep your scalpels away from me!' Her laugh was broken by a cough.

This seemed an excellent time to escape from the talkative woman and the nurse moving quickly to attend to her, both dismissing him as an unwelcome intruder. A dignified retreat was called for—but this hope was dashed as he encountered a plastic bin of sterile dressing packs waiting to catch his first step towards the exit. His muttered apology went unheard as he finally swerved towards the corridor.

The clatter of paper packets following the bin to the floor brought a sigh of annoyance from Catherine. All they needed was a disabled surgeon; she could only hope he didn't fall over everything in the operating theatre.

'The poor lad!' Mrs Murphy was sipping at a glass of water, eyed carefully by Catherine. Fluid intake was carefully rationed and monitored, and Mrs Murphy was quite likely to scoff the lot. 'Lovely looker, though, even with that gimpy leg.'

Taking away the nearly full glass, Catherine said, 'Well, that's probably the last we'll see of him over here.' She plumped up the pillows behind the patient's head. 'It's probably too far for him to walk anyway.'

As she settled back into a more comfortable position, Mrs Murphy smiled dreamily. 'Almost worth another go under the knife just to see them lovely eyes lookin' at you, so kind they are.'

Thinking that was a rather drastic means of gaining any man's attention, no matter how attractive, Catherine kept her peace. Few surgeons ever bothered them after their first visit; their unit was quite self-sufficient, and she was happy to keep it that way.

Glancing around the room, she nodded with satisfaction. Yes, they were quite capable of managing their patients without any interference. Except those plants did look a bit peaky; she hadn't really noticed. Maybe they needed a bit more light. She could do some pot tending in the afternoon. More water with some plant food should do the trick. No way would she take scissors to the pretty philodendron.

To Mrs Murphy's disappointment, Catherine's prediction proved accurate; there was no repeat visit from the new surgeon that week, and the routine of the dialysis unit continued without further disruption much as it had done for as long as they both could remember.

After the final patient had left for home on Friday afternoon, Catherine gathered up her sports bag and made her way to the staff recreation club. She had promised Emily that she would arrive early on Sunday, and it was in a mood of happy expectation of a relaxing and enjoyable weekend that she pushed open the door of the bar-cum-restaurant.

'Carlos, are you here?' she called.

There was no answer and no sign of the club manager, and Catherine stood still for a moment, looking around at the tables covered with multi-layered strands of coloured wires and light bulbs. Apparently Carlos was in the midst of yet another redecorating scheme.

She called again, and shrugged lightly at the lack of

response. He was probably attending to one of the other rooms, and she helped herself to a bottle of fresh orange juice from the bar before making space at one of the tables and settling herself to wait. If he didn't appear she could leave a note to add the drink to her monthly account.

It wasn't unusual to find the bar empty this early; most of the staff wouldn't arrive until the Happy Hour, but she would need Carlos to open up the indoor tennis court. Danny had insisted they needed the practice, and it was always fun to play with her long-time partner.

Her examination of the tangled wires on the table-top arising from the unsettling thought that they might be connected to an electric outlet was interrupted by loud exclamations in Spanish coming from outside. The manager had returned, but, whatever he was doing, something was blocking his entrance. Just as she was about to investigate, the door burst open and a tall metal trolley trundled through, accompanied by a gesticulating Carlos.

'Ah, this way, *señor*. Just a little bit more to the left. Ah, perfect! Careful, careful. Such a beauty! Careful. One more foot, *por favor*. Ah, *si*, this is perfect!'

Amused by the weaving progress of the heavy-wheeled vehicle carrying the largest and most colourful jukebox she had ever seen, Catherine watched as Carlos shoved chairs aside to find a place of honour by the wall. The centrepiece of his new décor had found its home. She applauded his efforts and waved her drink at him.

'Good! Just the person I wanted to see.'

Catherine's glance swerved around at the speaker and her jaw dropped. What was Matthew Dunnegan doing pushing recreation equipment around? Not that he didn't look the part, in his jeans and chequered shirt, rolled up to the elbows to display a formidable set of arm muscles that looked well suited to heaving deadweight objects around.

He was waving at her with a broad grin, and she quickly withdrew her upraised hand. He must have thought she was signalling to him!

'Be right with you. Just have to settle this *objet d'art*. OK, Carlos, *andelé*!' With one mighty shove Matthew Dunnegan lifted the machine from the trolley and staggered a few steps to where the manager was pointing.

'Many, many thanks, *señor*. This is where she will stay, my beauty.' The squat manager was beaming happily as he lovingly brushed the dusty curved edge of the battered jukebox. 'Soon she will be back to her true self, filled with colour and sound, you'll see.'

'If you say so.' The tall doctor grinned as he started to roll down his sleeves. He nodded to Catherine. 'Forgot my jacket and I need a bit of a wash and brush up. Won't be a sec.'

Wondering if she could make a quick escape from this unexpected encounter, Catherine decided to stay put. She had been here first, after all, and she was puzzled by something. There was something different about the new surgeon that she couldn't quite define. Without that shining white coat, he didn't look the same person. At least, he wasn't frowning, but there was something else.

Carlos had been distracted from his devotion to his latest addition by the arrival of new customers, and he disappeared into the kitchen. Catherine kept a hopeful eye on the arrivals; for once she was wishing Danny would get here on time.

'You got room for somebody else?' Matthew Dunnegan had reappeared, with damp strands of black hair falling over his forehead, edging the fine crinkles of his smiling face.

'Well. . . I'm waiting for someone.' The transformation really was quite remarkable, she thought. It must be the effect of that friendly grin, softening the firm lines of what was a highly sensual mouth. She jerked her thoughts away from this man's undeniable physical attractiveness, as a pile of tangled wire was being thrust across a chair.

'That's OK. So am I.' Having cleared a wider space, he looked at her empty bottle. 'Is this self-service?'

'Not really——'

'Here, Doctor. You like enchilada?' Carlos had reappeared, holding a steaming plate. 'You worked hard, so now you have earned a good meal.'

'Great! Smells terrific. Green chillies?' queried Matthew.

Ignoring the happy expectation in the doctor's response, Catherine frowned at the pub manager. He should know better than to try his trick with every new member. Before she could offer a warning Matthew Dunnegan had accepted the plate and was striding over to the bar for two large bottles of orange juice.

'How about these, Carlos?'

'On the house, Doctor. Enjoy your meal.' Bustling back to his duties, Carlos brushed aside any offer of payment.

It was when she saw Matthew Dunnegan walking rapidly back to the table that Catherine realised what was different. Her involuntary exclamation was one of surprised relief as well as puzzlement.

'You've lost it!'

CHAPTER TWO

MATTHEW stopped short, looked at the two bottles in his hands, then down at his feet before glancing at the table.

'Lost?'

Catherine immediately regretted her outburst. He must think she was daft. 'Sorry—I meant your limp. You've lost it.'

'Oh, that. A nuisance, but it's gone now.' He pushed one of the bottles towards her and eyed the waiting food appreciatively. 'I hope he uses tabasco.'

Catherine could have told him that Carlos used every spice in the book plus a generous helping of chillies, but she held her tongue. No one had yet survived more than one mouthful of the manager's speciality, and she waited for the spluttering that preceded the inevitable choked cry for liquid relief. She was to be disappointed.

Matthew Dunnegan tested the meat filling of one neatly rolled tortilla carefully and nodded. 'Not bad. Hepatitis.'

'What?' Carlos might have a heavy hand with the seasonings, but his kitchen was immaculate.

'The limp.' His mouth was filled with the chilli sauce and he swallowed before adding, 'Hepatitis B. Immunoglobulin shot. That staff nurse wields a needle like a flaming sword—damn near immobilised me. One of the unmentioned tribulations of life as a surgeon.' He speared another slice of tortilla.

Catherine could only nod, watching his demolition of the meat rolls with amazement. The man must have a cast-iron stomach; she was surprised a mere hypodermic could produce any sensation whatsoever. Wasn't there even a suspicion of watering in his eyes? No, that clear grey was unmarked by anything other than a gustatory pleasure, and now they were crinkling at the edges as he caught her glance.

'Want some? Sorry, I shouldn't have hogged the lot. Long time since I've had any of these.'

'No, thank you.' Deciding her drink would not be needed as balm for a scorched throat, Catherine poured it into her glass.

Matthew Dunnegan patted his abdomen with satisfaction. 'Great stuff! Now, Miss C. C., perhaps you can help with a few answers.'

Frowning into her glass, Catherine was silent. She had heard every variation possible on her name, but not this one, and she didn't like it any better than Cathy or Kate. Her eyes flickered over to the door. Danny was even later than usual.

'For instance,' Matthew continued, 'just how many of those dialysis patients have creatinine levels soaring through the roof?'

'I don't know——' Realising he was probably talking about Jackie's notes, she was confused. How could she answer such a question?

'Well, you should. Who sets the dialysis concentration levels?'

'We do, of course. It's been done like that——'

'Forever. I know.' His tone had become abrupt, and Catherine was reminded that even without his shining white coat, this was the outsider who knew nothing about how they ran their unit. 'And how many patients have haemoglobins in the cellar?'

'You're talking about Jackie.' She tried to focus on the one patient she knew best.

'Among others, I suspect.' He spoke quietly, gazing thoughtfully over her left shoulder. 'Thirteen beds, two sessions per day. About a hundred and thirty treatments a week for maybe fifty-odd patients.'

Catherine nodded. He had done the sums too quickly for her to follow, but it sounded right. She didn't know whether to be glad or sorry that he had shown enough interest to check the figures. 'We also cover for dialysis on the wards, intensive therapy and so on.'

'Sure, but of those fifty-odd patients coming in every week how many have been on the books for more than two years?'

Catherine thought back. Their last new patient had been Mr Petrussi. 'All of them,' she said.

Matthew's expression remained bland. 'Including Jackie.' His voice deepened. 'You've had a ten-year-old child on peritoneal dialysis for the last two years?'

She was beginning to feel uncomfortable under this cross-examination. 'I told you—there was no matching donor.'

He leaned forward, his words laced with anger. 'Even if there were, she's in no fit state for a transplant. She's severely anaemic, the urea and creatinine levels are god-awful, and no surgeon in his right mind would consider her as a patient with even half a chance of avoiding rejection.'

'At least she's alive!' Catherine protested.

'Barely.' There was a deceptive softness in his voice. 'That's no life for a child, hooked up to dialysis bags for hours on end, and it isn't doing her much good at that.' He paused. 'Why no EPO?'

'Because we haven't got any!' Catherine felt as if her body had been fixed on a pin and he was about to start pulling her wings off. 'Our unit can't get it. It's too expensive.'

'At least you know what it is, even if not a single patient is getting what could clear up most of those anaemias I can see without looking at their notes.'

'Of course I know what it is! All chronic renal failure patients are deficient in erythropoetin.' Did he think she was completely ignorant as well as being responsible for all the inadequacies of their overstretched and understaffed unit?

'Has the aptly named Mrs Blessington been approached about getting funds, if that's the reason why EPO isn't being prescribed?' Matthew persisted.

Catherine sighed. There was a lot he didn't know about how the system worked. 'Donors and volunteer fund-raisers want something specific for their charitable efforts, preferably with gold plaques attached. They need something they can see, and we need new equipment just as much as we need everything else.'

'You do indeed, Miss C. C. There sure is a lot needed around here.' His voice had lightened and the firm mouth was softening into the barest hint of a smile. He leaned back and kept his eyes on her face.

For some reason, his change of mood made Catherine uneasy. His irritation at frustrations they all knew was at least understandable; she felt on safer ground when he was openly attacking. 'And I suppose you think *you* can solve everything just like magic? Everyone will suddenly take up their beds and walk, leaving all the drip poles and trailing tubes?'

She bit her lip. Maybe she had gone too far, but he was provoking her, with that holier-than-thou attitude, criticising everything they did. He really was too full of himself, as if he had the answers no one else had been able to find.

Watching for a return of those lowered brows that meant more argument, Catherine braced herself.

Matthew Dunnegan refused the bait and his lips began to curve into a teasing grin. 'Not exactly, no. But someone ought to take things in hand.' At that instant his fingers closed over hers, and Catherine could feel the quicksand threatening the ground under her feet. Trying to ignore the lovely warmth that was seeping up her arm, she made no effort to retrieve her hand. He wouldn't have the satisfaction of making her back away.

'Surgeons,' she said slowly, surprised at how calm her voice sounded, 'have no right to interfere with the dialysis unit. What we do is none of your business. We can run our own affairs without your interference.'

His hand maintained an even pressure that prevented her from curling her fingers away from him. 'That's not the way I see it, Miss C. C. It's my job to get those people off those beds and away from your machines. It's a sort of body repair work, you might say.'

'Why do you call me that?' she queried. The delicious tingling in the tips of her fingers was making it difficult to concentrate on what he was saying.

'Miss C. C? Just a mnemonic—a way of remembering. C. C.—crooked cap. Easy.'

'Oh!' She could feel a flush of embarrassment creeping up her neck. 'We. . .we don't wear them very often, only when visitors are around.'

'Well, I'm not exactly a visitor, and I think I intend to interfere.' His smile broadened. 'Yes, indeedy, a little interference might be just what's called for around here.'

'Why can't you leave us alone?' Catherine cried out sharply as she tried to move her fingers. To her surprise he suddenly released her, and watched as she instinctively moved to straighten a cap she wasn't wearing.

'I never could resist a challenge.' There was a twinkling glint in his eyes as he grinned at her obvious discomfiture. 'You ought to let it down, you know.'

She shot him a glare from under lowered lashes, but she doubted it would divert his rapt attention with her fumbling attempts to straighten what felt like a mass of tangled hair. She wondered if she looked as flustered as she felt; certainly her fingers were not responding as they should, and she abandoned her efforts to hide them under the table.

Matthew Dunnegan gave every appearance of enjoying her confusion. 'All that glorious red—probably a sign of a temper, but I can live with that. Yup, it's definitely a sin to hide away that fiery loveliness.' He ignored her attempt to interrupt. 'I'm going to need your help with what I've got in mind.'

'Help?' The word came out as a high squeak; his foolish flattery had been unexpected. She lowered her voice to growl, 'What plans?'

'Got to get things moving around here.' He leaned across suddenly and frowned into her face before nodding to himself. 'Green—I knew it! It had to be green.' He straightened up again. 'Can't have everybody around here sitting on their backsides. It's definitely time for a little action.'

He sounded light hearted, but there was an undertone of determination Catherine was beginning to recognise. 'What are you planning, exactly?' she asked suspiciously.

'Oh—'

Before he could answer there was a crackling explosion behind his back, followed by the sound of splintering glass.

'What—?' Catherine had jumped at the sound and half rose.

'It's all right.' After one swift glance over his shoulder, Matthew grasped her wrists in his lean fingers and gently sat her down. 'No problem. Our friend Carlos is just experimenting with his beauty. Pushed his luck, and she got a bit sparky. I know the feeling.' He patted her hands lightly. 'Hopefully no harm done.'

Withdrawing from his touch, Catherine watched as

several customers moved to help clean up the broken panel from the jukebox. Carlos must have tried to connect the electrical plug, and now there was a jagged hole in the façade showing dust-covered metal workings usually hidden behind the coloured lights.

'A little tape and glue and she'll be as good as new.' Matthew glanced at the shattered fragments.

Catherine could feel her pulse rate scudding erratically; sudden noises were always a shock to the system, but she wasn't usually so easily upset. The man across from her had shown very fast reflexes, and he didn't look the least concerned at what could have been a narrow escape. She tried to smile. 'More body repair work, I suppose.'

'Exactly.' His laugh was rich and deep and oddly reassuring above the clamour of worried voices; others turned to the sound and smiled in response. 'She'll reward his care and devotion if he treats her with respect, now he knows she tends to explode occasionally.'

Not caring to examine any double meanings in his words, Catherine watched a vaguely familiar staff member approaching their table.

'Are you Mr Dunnegan?' At Matthew's nod, the man pointed back to the door. 'There's someone asking for you.'

'Right, thanks.' Sliding smoothly from behind the table, Matthew paused to lift his jacket from the back of his chair. Before Catherine could move he leaned down and brushed her chin with his thumb. 'Now there are little glints of gold in the green. Lovely!' His thumb feathered lightly across her lips. 'See you, Miss C. C.'

There was no time for her to respond before he disappeared through the milling crowd with a stride that seemed to carry him with an inner propulsion impossible to deflect. As she fingered her lips reflectively, Catherine watched as he greeted a petite dark-haired girl, placing his arm around her shoulder.

'From one to another,' she muttered to herself. 'Can't say he wastes any time!' Wondering precisely what his unstated plans might be, it was impossible to doubt he would carry them out, brooking no opposition. Matthew Dunnegan was a man used to getting whatever he wanted. It might be interesting to see what he would do if everything, or everyone, did not fall in with his schemes.

She was still sitting in silent reverie when Danny finally found her.

'Sorry I'm late, Cath. Some idiot medic wanted copies of all the transplant tissue typings for the past year. Would you believe it?'

Catherine could well believe it, and had a strong suspicion as to who had ordered such an onerous review. 'Did everyone have to stay?' she asked.

Her tennis partner's usually friendly face was gloomy. 'Even the Chief. The whole lab's in uproar. Just wait till we find out who thought this up for a Friday afternoon!'

Smiling to herself, Catherine waved to Carlos and hefted her sports bag to her shoulder. Maybe Matthew Dunnegan had managed to antagonise the renal technicians, and that should put a spanner in the works. She flexed her fingers experimentally. 'Let's go, Danny. We can pretend the busybody doctor is the opposition and smash him until he begs for mercy.'

'Fine by me.' Danny was eyeing the empty plate on the table. 'You didn't eat one of Carlos's specials, did you?' He eyed her in respectful surprise.

'Not me.' She called over her shoulder, 'Just some person with no sense of taste. No sense, no feeling and armour-plated innards. I've got the key.' Without waiting, she led the way to the court, where she intended to vent a good deal of energy on defenceless tennis balls whose behaviour she could usually predict.

An energetic practice session did provide release for pent-up feelings; she and Danny were playing together better than they ever had. Surely this year they would win back their trophy in the staff tournament. Few players could withstand Danny's backhand, and her own serve had improved. Neither of them doubted that the current champions would have to give up their silver cup.

The arrival of the post on Saturday morning brought an added delight to the sense of wellbeing Catherine felt. There were two postcards and an airmail package addressed in familiar handwriting.

The first card, a picture of snowbound Alpine ridges, was from her mother stating how well her father was doing in his search of archive material for his book on early timepieces, and the second, sporting a sepia drawing of a medieval water clock, was in her father's spidery scrawl describing her mother's splendid work with watercolour studies of the mountains. Catherine added them to a large collection of their counterparts on her bulletin board. Her parents were happily progressing across Europe as well as her wall; some things never changed, and she was as content as they were to have it that way.

It was the contents of the small packet that sent her scurrying off to the shops. Such a perfect gift deserved a complementary ensemble, and Catherine did not regret spending half a month's salary to do justice to the intricately traced golden earrings.

Touching the ragged writing paper covered with the large upright lettering so similar to her own, she smiled at the succinct message. *Thinking of you. Love, M.*

'Me too,' she whispered. He might be halfway around the world, but Mark was always a part of her.

He had known how much she would love the exotic drops, in the shape of intertwined stems enclosing a single freshwater pearl.

She couldn't be so certain about the results of her spending spree. Twisting around in front of the full-length mirror, she examined her loose cream and brown tunic with critical eyes. Chocolate-brown opaque tights made the above-knee hemline less daring than it might have been, but she had doubts about the new flat shoes. Wiggling her toes against the supple tan leather, Catherine grinned at herself. Pixie boots. There was nothing elfin about the long legs clearly visible beneath the exceedingly short dress.

'Well, it's the fashion, and it is Josh's birthday, after all.' She wiggled her hips to feel the soft wool flowing against her body. 'And very comfortable.' The polo collar helped to draw attention to the precious earrings.

It was true, she decided. There were definite green glints in the widely spaced hazel eyes staring back from her reflection. She blinked to make them disappear; they made her look like a goggle-eyed cat. There, that was better. Now the shining pearls reflected a softer brown, and a gold hairclip would help. There was no sense in leaving her unruly waves loose to hide the one touch of glamour she possessed, and she resolutely swept up her shoulder-length hair into a neat coil.

Covering the mini-dress with her long camel coat, Catherine was grateful for the looseness around her legs as she ran to catch the early Sunday bus to Emily's house. The carefully wrapped present was stashed in her shoulder-bag and helped to keep her knees safely hidden under the coat as she luxuriated in the freshness of the clear morning air and the empty roads leading to the outskirts of the town.

Her monthly visits were always a kind of homecoming, and she knew how lucky she was to have such good friends who allowed her to share their lives as if she were an extended family member. She loved their rambling old house almost as much as they did. There was a sense of security and stability about the tree-lined street and tidy privet hedges hugging the large plots, keeping the occupiers safe and snug.

Hoping the weather would stay warm enough to allow her to do some weeding and digging in the large back garden, Catherine watched for her bus stop. Emily never had the time to take care of the crowded herbaceous borders, and Catherine took a special pleasure in clearing out the undergrowth, as a small contribution to the family chores.

As she approached the familiar house, the reason for Emily's fully occupied time came hurtling out with a welcoming shriek.

'Auntie Cath!'

Two small arms held her legs in a surprisingly strong arm lock, and Catherine leaned down laughingly to tousle the dark head burrowing near her coat pocket. 'Hi, Seth. No, I didn't forget, but you leave my bag alone! That's for your daddy.'

She pulled out a small package of oat biscuits and allowed him to start nibbling at the edges before calling out, 'Anybody home?'

'In here, Catherine.' Emily's voice came closer. 'Seth, you leave her be!' As her broadly smiling face appeared in the hallway, Emily added, 'He's still at that terrible two stage. Nothing keeps him still for long. Come on in.'

'I've brought some fruit. The market had gorgeous mandarins, even pomegranates.'

Emily hugged Catherine. 'You don't have to bring anything, you know. The Christmas goodies are out already; I can barely even think about it yet.'

'Where's Josh?' Catherine followed her friend into the hall after hanging up her coat.

'Up in the loft. . .wow! Where did you get that?' Emily's eyes widened as she took in the new dress. 'And short! It's great, Catherine. Really makes you look sexy. Who's it all in aid of, I ask myself?' Her brows raised questioningly. 'Not our Danny, surely? Turn round and let me see.'

Catherine laughed and reluctantly twirled quickly. 'I just gave myself a present. It's really warm.'

'Oh, sure. For warmth you get a thermal vest, not this. Do you think short people like me could wear something like that? At least it's loose enough.'

'Anybody could.' Feeling self-conscious, Catherine looked around the kitchen. 'Do you need any help?' She noticed neatly cut circles of mince laid out on a tray.

'Today is hamburgers. It's Josh's idea but he hasn't even set up the barbecue yet.' Emily called over the open stairwell leading to the top floor. 'Josh! Come on down, Catherine's here, and you haven't ——'

The sound of rapidly descending footsteps were drowned in the excited voice of Emily's husband. 'Hey, have you seen what's coming up the street? Take a look, Em. It really is something!'

'What are you talking about?' Emily sounded surprised. Josh rarely got this active about anything on Sundays.

The thin frame of Josh Beatty appeared at the foot of the stairs. 'Come and look. Hi, Catherine. I've never seen anything like this in our neighbourhood. Wonder where it's going?' By the time he finished speaking he had disappeared into the front room, and the two women followed, after exchanging surprised glances.

'Maybe he's lost or something,' said Catherine.

They followed where Josh was pointing, towards a

very old, very large automobile inching slowly up the
street.

'Now who can know anybody with one of those
things? Maybe there's a wedding near here.' Emily
stared out of the crisp white curtains. 'It's an old
Roller! Look, Catherine. He's slowing down. . .oh!'

As the great silver car gradually slowed to a stop
outside the path leading to the Beattys' front door,
Josh backed away from the window to run outside. The
tall figure emerging from the driver's door was only too
familiar to Catherine.

'What's *he* doing here?' she gasped.

'Well. . . I forgot to tell you.' Emily kept her eyes
on the two men shaking hands beside the shining car.
'We got to talking in the canteen and he said he was
longing for some decent food, and Josh says any Yank
can get withdrawal symptoms without decent hamburgers and—well,' she turned with a sheepish grin, 'I
didn't think you'd mind, really.'

'I'm surprised he didn't bring a friend.' Catherine
remembered the petite girl with the neat dark bob.

'Oh, no. He doesn't know anybody yet, and lives all
by himself in a grotty basement flat.'

'How do you know that?' asked Catherine.

'I told you, we got to talking. Oh, what are they
doing now?' Emily had turned back to see her husband
slip in behind the wheel with a wide smile as their
visitor stood back. Now the ancient Rolls-Royce was
being sedately driven up their drive and into the
anonymity of the empty garage. 'Well! I hope he didn't
hit his bicycle.' She grinned at Catherine. 'Adds a little
class to the Beatty house, don't you think?'

At this moment Catherine was not thinking very
clearly at all. As the sound of the men's voices neared
the house, she was aware only of an overwhelming
feeling of vexation with Matthew Dunnegan. He

seemed to be everywhere she went, and now here. He was invading even this haven of peacefulness; her thoughts of a pleasurable Sunday were rapidly evaporating.

She could hear Josh talking like an excited boy, and she darted back into the kitchen, searching for an apron, the bigger the better.

'That was great, Matt — really terrific! Never thought I'd get to sit in one of those. It's a '65 Silver Cloud Three, isn't it? Just like the old movies!'

'I don't know about that, Josh. It's only rented. Said they didn't have——'

Emily interrupted, 'You know Catherine, Matt.'

Catherine turned slowly as the familiar voice filled the kitchen, noting absently that the two men were already on a first-name basis. She kept her voice cool. 'Hello, Mr Dunnegan.'

CHAPTER THREE

'CATHERINE.' He spoke her name slowly as if savouring each syllable. 'Lovely!' His eyes moved with purposeful deliberation from the tips of her shoes to the shining clip at the top of her head, pausing at the sparkling drops glinting in the sun and coming to rest on the crushed apron clenched in her fists. 'All golden.'

A small voice piped up, ''Lo. I'm Seth.'

With a quiet sigh, Matthew Dunnegan allowed his glance to move away from Catherine and he smiled at the boy. 'Hello, Seth. How de do?' He shook the tiny hand solemnly.

'Auntie Cath. . .prezzie.'

'Ah, yes. Well, your Auntie Cath. . .' his eyebrows rose, but he did not look at Catherine '. . .is more of a regular visitor, I gather.' And none too pleased at the addition of another guest, he added to himself. To the child he said, 'There might be something of interest in the old banger. Shall we look?'

'Yah!' With a squeal of delight, Seth allowed himself to be hoisted towards the ceiling on Matthew's shoulder, but before they could leave the kitchen Josh came in, carrying a bulging carrier bag.

'What's all this, Matt? Did you think we wouldn't feed you?'

'You did say burgers. I just brought a few extra fixings, that's all.'

Emily had reached for the bag and began to unload a variety of jars and plastic containers. She held up a large bottle, and laughed as her son made a grab for it. 'Even pickled onions! You'll make one member of this household sick—he has a passion for them! All right, just one and off you go. Josh, take Matt and the little pickle-eater outside. If you don't fix that grill, we don't eat!'

During this exchange Catherine had wrapped herself in a voluminous cotton apron and busied herself with sorting out cutlery. Her cheeks felt as if they were aflame, and she could still sense that searching gaze, as if he had imprinted every inch of her on his memory. It was the earrings; she shouldn't have worn them, but it was too late now. After Matthew Dunnegan left the kitchen there at least seemed room to breathe. 'How can we eat all of this?' she queried.

'He's even brought a home-made barbecue sauce!' Emily was sorting out the condiments. 'Just what we needed. Isn't he clever?'

'Very.' Catherine eyed the unlabelled glass jar suspiciously. It was probably filled with inedible chillies.

Emily gave her friend a quizzical smile. 'He certainly noticed the new you!' After a pause she added, 'You're putting corn relish into the salad bowl, Catherine. Not such a good idea, really.'

'Oh, I'm sorry. I just. . .' Catherine stammered. 'I wasn't expecting him, that's all.' She looked at the profusion of pickles, relishes and sauces arrayed on the counter. 'I don't know what to do with all this.'

'Then leave it to me. You can go outside and keep Seth out of their way if they're trying to put that old contraption together. Shoo!'

Reluctantly, Catherine picked up a tray of clean plates covered with a cloth and carried it towards the sound of loud male laughter interspersed with clanging metal and childish squeals. The Beatty home was usually much quieter; the new visitor had brought noise and activity along with his groceries.

Both men were sitting cross-legged in front of the scattered parts of the unassembled barbecue.

'Does this bit fit in here?' Matt was examining a wide grill with metal attachments.

Josh was tightening screws on the base of a rectangular apparatus. 'God only knows. Mechanical things defeat me. Give me computers any day—much more sensible things; they don't need muscle power. Ah!'

'Watch it! You don't want to lose a finger.' The surgeon eyed the small cut with a professional eye. 'Computers, eh?' He looked up as Catherine arrived and grinned. 'Good timing. A nurse's attention is required here. First aid for the barbecue builder.'

Grateful to have a practical reason for being there, Catherine took a look at Josh's hand. 'You could use a plaster,' she said. 'Are there any inside?'

'I know where they are. You stay put.' Josh stood up and said to Matt, 'Don't you try and do it all by yourself. After all, those hands of yours are a lot more important than mine. Won't be a jiff.'

With Josh's departure Catherine again felt ill at ease. Looking for Seth, she could see him curled up on a lounge chair looking sleepy. There would be no diversion there. Absentmindedly she picked up the instruction sheets abandoned by Josh.

'If you read those out I should be able to get this thing working,' said Matthew.

Catherine tried to focus on the creased paper, but the diagrams were indecipherable. 'He's right, you know,' she said.

'About what?' Matthew Dunnegan watched her carefully, a pastime he found thoroughly delightful.

'About your hands.' She looked up swiftly, then returned her attention to the meaningless lines, arrows and letters in her hands. 'Losing a finger would make your life difficult.'

'Hurdles are meant to be overcome.' He shrugged. 'Read on. What do I do with this grill bit?'

Thinking of several unpleasant suggestions she might make, Catherine frowned, looked at the sections on the ground and shook her head.

'Maybe if you turned it right side up?'

Inwardly groaning at her own muddle-headedness, Catherine twisted the sheet around. This man was having an unfortunate effect on her thought processes. 'There. Over there, that sticking-out bit. It hinges on, I think.'

'Right, whatever you say, Miss C. C.'

'Don't call me that!'

'All right, Catherine, I won't.' His eyes were crinkling at her again as an easy smile played at the corners of his mouth.

The effect of that smile was alarming and not the least bit conducive to clear thinking. Catherine took a deep breath and steadied her hands; the air temperature in the garden seemed to have risen in the past few minutes, and she gave herself a mental shake. Stop behaving like a silly schoolgirl! she thought.

There was a delicious aroma of spiced musk on the morning air blending with the clove scent of late-blooming pinks at the edge of the patio. It was definitely time to concentrate on the task at hand. She picked up a nearby metal rod. 'Try this,' she said.

The rod was heavier than it looked, and her wrist buckled as she tried to lift it.

'Whoa, there!' A large hand closed over hers. 'I'd rather you didn't wave that weapon around quite so freely, if you don't mind. A finger I can live without— an absent eye is quite another matter.' His grasp had slid up her arm in a widening circle of pressure, and as Catherine tried to flex her fingers the slim rod slipped out of her nerveless hand.

'That's better. Safer anyway.' Matt grinned as he
released her hand, balancing the rod against his palm
as if it weighed less than a feather. 'This might do it.
Let's find out.'

His head bent in concentration, and Catherine
watched a swath of the dark wavy hair fall casually
across his forehead. From this angle his face looked
quite different; the stubborn angular jaw was hidden
by the shadow of that high-bridged nose. She found
the irregular outline fascinating. There was a definite
bump, right in the middle. Had someone broken this
man's nose at some time in the past?

The thought made her smile. Maybe he'd been a
tough little boy, always fighting to get his own way and
ending up grubby and dirty but probably victorious. A
muttered grunt broke into this rather appealing picture,
and Catherine switched her attention to the man's
hands as the long fingers felt around the tip of the
shaft, searching for the exact fit to make the connection
that would hold firm.

Her own sigh echoed his as he slid the rod into
position and held it a moment before locking it into
place. 'There, that should last.' Wrapping his fingers
around the completed attachment, Matt pulled sharply.
The join held.

'There we are, my beauty! Should last a lifetime.'

His smile of satisfaction was infectious, and
Catherine met his glance with a slight twitch of her
own lips. Not even hardened metal could withstand
those knowledgeable and determined hands. 'Yes, it
looks fine,' she agreed.

'Hey, you've done it!' Josh had reappeared and was
regarding his completed barbecue with a pleased smile.
He was holding both his hands behind his back and
there was a hint of embarrassment in his voice as he

asked, 'Hey, Matt, are you—I mean, your name is Dunnegan, right?'

Matt nodded as his eyes returned to examine his handiwork. 'Yeah, fourth generation Yankee Irish, that's me. Looks all right, doesn't it?' He aimed an experimental kick at the structure. 'Shouldn't fall over.'

'No, it's great. I mean, you're Matt Dunnegan. *The* Matt Dunnegan?'

The grey eyes twinkled at Josh's expression. 'Well, my mother would say so.'

'No, I mean. . .the College Bowl. . . Old Miss. You're Miracle Matt!'

Any response was lost as Emily bustled in, carrying a tray piled high with meat patties. 'The salad is coming later after you've started cooking.' She looked at her husband. 'Well, have you shown him yet?'

'No, not yet.' Josh smiled sheepishly as he pulled a dilapidated football from behind his back. 'Look, Matt—I got this the year you won the Bowl. MVP and all. Best hands ever, the best. See, it's got all the signatures, even yours!'

'That was a long time ago, Josh.' Holding the dusty treasure carefully, Matt smilingly shook his head. 'Ancient history.'

'Only eight years.' Josh had settled beside the tall man on the grass. 'I was a lowly Freshman and you were a Senior. I used to watch all the team practices and dream the impossible.' His face was bright with memories. 'Me, the skinny kid, running a Liberty play for Matt Dunnegan. Remember your final Hail Mary throw in the play-offs?'

'Josh! I won't have that kind of language!' Emily spoke sharply and pointed at the barbecue. 'If you don't get started on the cooking, we'll all fade away from lack of food.'

'Aw, Em. . .!'

'It's OK, Josh. Let's wash up and create wonders for the ladies.' Matt unwound himself from his cross-legged position and handed back the football. 'You can hang on to this. Those glory days are long gone now. Where did we put that special sauce?'

Moving to help Emily sort out the plates and cutlery, Catherine watched Josh cradle the old ball under his arms and zig-zag dramatically across the patio to the kitchen door. 'What's all that about?' she queried.

'Memories of college days, heaven help us! Apparently Matt was the team quarterback or something and his personal hero.' Emily smiled ruefully. 'I haven't seen Josh so excited since he got his first bubble jet printer!' She unwrapped a plastic container. 'I probably should have put a football on this, but there was hardly enough room for the candles.'

The birthday cake was decorated with a colourful iced reproduction of a toy train, and as she did a rapid count of the twenty-six wobbly candles, Catherine remembered. 'Oh, I left his present in my bag—I'll have to get it.'

'Can you bring the shoebox from beside the coat rack with you? That's the one place he never looks.' Emily arranged the cake in a central position of honour, deftly preventing her sleepy son from touching it.

The only way of avoiding being seen was to use the lounge, and Catherine was grateful for the loud voices in the kitchen as she retrieved the hidden parcels. Both men were deep in conversation and she hurried back just before they emerged, still talking.

'What do you mean, get into another program?' Josh was asking. 'That's illegal over here, just like everywhere else, so far as I know.'

'Even if you have the right whatever. . .password?' Matt was sporting an oversized plastic apron embellished with a comical caricature of a carrot-crunching rabbit.

'Well, no, I guess not. But the code has to be personalised, you know. If it's not yours legally, you're hacking into somebody else's program, and that's not such a good idea. Do we have any tinfoil?'

'Allow me.' Matt examined the neat roll of meat patties and reached for the unlabelled jar. 'Needs an expert touch, this. Just the right amount.' His eyes fell on the cake. 'Nobody told me this was a birthday.'

Josh grinned. 'Another one for me. You must be near the dreaded big three-oh.'

'Getting close.' Matt turned his attention to the grill and deftly slipped a spatula under the first circle of meat. 'Do we have a pastry brush or a spoon?'

'Here you are.' Emily was watching his movements with approval; he was much more skilled than her husband. She added, without looking at her friend, 'We usually have it later and combine it with Catherine's birthday. They're the same age, but she chickened out this year.'

As she turned to glare at Emily, Catherine caught Matt's brief glance; there was a definite twinkle in those grey depths. She stifled her embarrassment and willed him to say nothing. She would deal with Emily later.

Matt had not missed the quick flush on Catherine's cheeks. As much as he appreciated Emily Beatty's efforts, he could wish for a touch more subtlety. 'So tell me then, Josh, how do I get a program I want?' he asked.

'Buy the right software, I suppose. What have you got?' Josh sniffed deeply as the spicy aroma began to permeate the garden. 'Just like home, that smell.' He nodded at his wife. 'This is the real thing, this is.'

'The first one for the hostess, for her judgement.'

Matt slipped the first burger into a bun and waited for Emily's reaction.

'Mmm, it's really good, Matt,' Emily nodded after the first bite.

As he flipped another patty, adding a generous dollop of sauce, Matt spoke through a hiss of steam. 'I don't know enough about computers, Josh. I've got a working terminal, but it doesn't give me the information I want.' He was silent for a moment before he slid the next burger into a warm roll and held it out for Catherine. 'There's a lot more I need to know before I'll get what I want.'

His warm smile was having an unusual effect on her digestive processes, as Catherine felt her stomach flutter expectantly. It must be simple hunger, and she looked for the nearest jug of juice; he had been more than liberal with that sauce of his. She took a tentative nibble of the crusty roll and felt the tangy juice tickle her mouth and throat. It was the most delicious hamburger she had ever tasted, and involuntarily her tongue tip licked at her top lip to catch any furtive drop of flavour.

A deep chuckle greeted her response, and Matt turned his attention to speeding up the cooking under Josh's impatient gaze. 'Does your company sell software?' he asked.

'Yeah, sure.' Josh was ready with his empty plate. 'Do you mean you want to buy something special?'

'Don't know yet. Could be.' Ladling two burgers on to the waiting plate, Matt quickly added two more to the grill. 'I could use some expert help. Don't suppose you could take a look?'

'Yeah, sure.' Josh was mumbling through his munching. 'Just say the word. Don't forget your pickled onions.'

'Not on your life!' Matt was settling himself and all

conversation ceased as the serious eating began. As soon as one plate was emptied, the efficient chef had a replacement ready, and it was several minutes before Emily finally held up her hand.

'I'm beginning to burst, and we've still got the cake to go.' She shifted her son's weight on her lap. 'And I know someone who wants a taste of all that icing!'

Muted groans greeted her suggestion, and Catherine made a move to retrieve the hidden parcels. 'Don't forget the presents.' When she tried to sit up she found her centre of gravity seemed to have shifted somewhere towards her feet; she had eaten far too much, but it had been impossible to refuse after that first delectable taste.

'Great grub and now prezzies—what more could a man ask for?' Josh eyed the carefully wrapped boxes. 'I've seen that shoebox somewhere before.'

As he opened each parcel and made appropriate remarks about the carefully knitted scarf and gloves from his wife and the crayon drawing from his son, Josh did not notice that Matt had moved away and started tidying up the remnants of the feast. 'Now this is great, Seth.' He reached over to hug the boy as he wrapped the new woollens around the small body.

'That's for your rides into work on the bike.' Emily handed him Catherine's parcel. 'I'm always practical, but we couldn't forget your toys.'

The two women giggled at each other; this had been a joint effort. Catherine said, 'It had better be the right kind, it took us long enough to figure it all out.'

Josh let out a long happy sigh as the paper revealed its secret—an intricately work-detailed miniature steam locomotive. 'Hey, Matt, lookee here! It's a Golden Eagle!' He grinned at Catherine. 'And it's even the right gauge! Thanks a lot, it's great.'

Pleased with his delight, Catherine happily watched

as he playfully ran it up and down his son's leg. To her surprise, Matt left his work and came to hunch down beside Josh.

'She's a real beauty, Josh. Even got a firebox.' There was a childlike longing in his voice, and Catherine exchanged a glance with Emily. Surely there couldn't be another model train fanatic as bad as Josh?

'You know models, Matt?'

'Yeah. We. . . I used to have one of those multi-tracked jobs. The engine had red wheels. It was all black, not like this.' Matthew traced one fingertip along the edge of the bright green and blue paint. 'It even had a whistle.'

Josh lifted his son on to his shoulder as he said, 'Spoken like a true connoisseur! Shall we show him our set-up, Seth? We've got four tracks, but it's the signals that are the best, eh?'

Emily gave an exaggerated groan. 'Before you disappear into the loft, you can at least put your son to bed for his nap.' Turning to Catherine, she added, 'There's no hope for it—boys will unfortunately be boys.'

There was a wistful look on Matthew Dunnegan's face that Catherine found oddly touching; he was yearning to play with the shiny toy she had spent so much time choosing, little thinking it would give such obvious pleasure to a man she didn't know. For a moment she found herself wondering how much else there was to know about this unpredictable man who would scowl as readily as he smiled, who took over in every situation, riding roughshod over anyone else's wishes or opinions, but who could look comically apologetic just because he wanted to play with a new friend's train set.

'Is it OK, Emily? We can do the dishes first.'

Both women smiled at the polite offer from Matt.

Josh was already halfway to the kitchen door, and Emily waved the tall man after him. 'Go on, both of you. Now Josh has someone to play with, and it is his birthday, after all!'

With a deliberate effort, Catherine hoisted herself out of the cosy lounge chair and began to help Emily clear away the dishes. The cake had barely been touched, and she wrapped it carefully.

'Listen, why don't you leave me to the clearing up.' Emily was piling crockery on a tray. 'Then you can enjoy pottering around the garden, what's left of it. Today everybody should do just what they want, and I have to check on Seth anyway, Josh never takes time to read him a story.' She cocked an ear upwards. 'And I can hear the motors starting.'

True enough, there was a distant humming sound interspersed with soft clicking and a brief muted whistle as if coming from far, far away. As she looked around the neglected flower beds Catherine heard the plaintive call again, this time drawn out as if a finger had prolonged the shrill solitary note.

Even model train whistles had an eerie sound, she thought, and was relieved to have a gust of wind bring the remote sound of male voices to her ears. Obviously the two men were settling for an afternoon of juvenile activity, and she took a closer look at the last flowering rose bush. It was in sad need of pruning, as were the borders on the edge of the patio.

Perhaps she could just sit for a while and examine the possibilities. It really was such a glorious warm afternoon that physical work did not seem so appealing. It was enough just to look and smell and feel the peace of the day. And hear it, she thought as the strains of a rollicking song drifted down from the top of the house. Something about a Casey Jones on his

way to the promised land. Most of the words were
indistinct, but they sounded cheerful.

She closed her eyes slightly and watched the lambent
light play through her lashes, misting the edges of the
coral-coloured roses. This must be close to being the
promised land, she thought sleepily as she watched a
fat bee scurry for the end of the season's nectar. The
warmth on her face was soothing, and there was only
one vague thought that troubled her. She strained to
hear the words, but the wind was taking them away.
What on earth was a Wabash Cannonball? she wondered drowsily.

Something was brushing at her cheek, and she flicked
at it with irritation.

'Rise and shine, Sleeping Beauty! It's time we were
going.'

'What. . .?' Catherine blinked. A pair of amused
grey eyes was all she could see, and she tried to wave
away the obstacle. The dream had been lovely—
something about fluffy rose-coloured balls floating
towards an enchanted land of milk and honey filled
with lovely singing. 'Go away. . .'

'Nope.'

Catherine struggled to surface from the clinging
tentacles of her beautiful imaginings; it was much too
warm and cosy, and she began to sink back into the
welcoming cocoon.

'Ups-a-daisy!' With a start, she felt herself being
bodily lifted.

'Go away! I don't want——'

'All good things must come to an end, and it's time
to go home.'

Now her eyes were wide open and she seemed to be
holding Matthew Dunnegan around the neck. Quickly
she let go and tried to sit up, letting the jacket slide

off. Jacket? Looking down, Catherine saw the light-weight leather coat Matt had been wearing. Someone must have put it over her while she was asleep. 'Oh! What time is it?'

'You were absolutely zonked!' This sounded like Josh, and Catherine looked across at him. How long had they been sitting there?

'Time we were on our way.' Matt had retrieved his jacket and slung it around his shoulders. 'My sense of direction is muddled enough in the daylight, and it's starting to get dark.'

Catherine felt distinctly grumpy and dishevelled. 'What do you mean, we?' she demanded. She was perfectly capable of using a bus; again he was taking things for granted. The glimpse of charming child had disappeared. 'Are you finished playing trains?'

'Yeah, it was great, Catherine. Best birthday I ever had.' Now Josh was speaking with boyish excitement. 'Can I take the Rolls out, Matt?'

'Sure, be my guest.' Matthew kept his eyes on Catherine's face, still flushed from sleep. 'Just watch the accelerator, though. It seemed a bit tricky to me.'

The strong fingers under her elbow were steering her firmly into the house, and Catherine fumbled with her apron strings. Her brain was still fuzzy, but she could recognise when she was being manoeuvred against her own inclinations. 'Really, I. . .' she began.

Now her coat was being wrapped around her, held in place under a warm grasp. 'Your chariot awaits, madam.'

'I'm so jealous Catherine,' Emily said as she pushed them through the front door. 'Isn't it grand-looking?'

The gleaming silver car filled the small drive as Josh stood aside in admiration. Catherine could feel the twitching of net curtains across the street; there could hardly be a more ostentatious form of transport. Matt was standing by the right-hand side, waiting.

She glared at him. 'Do you expect me to drive this thing?' she demanded.

'Whoops—forgot!' He moved smoothly around to the opposite side to hold the door open.

Watched by her approving friends, she didn't have much choice other than to obey. As she sank into the luxuriously upholstered seat a heady smell of old leather and polished hardwood engulfed her senses. She eyed the shining circular dials as Matt slid behind the steering-wheel.

'Do you know how to drive this monster?' she asked.

'Sort of.'

There was time only for a brief wave to Emily and Josh before the great car responded to the driver's command and roared off in a surge of controlled power.

CHAPTER FOUR

'HERE, take this.'

'What is it?' Catherine asked automatically. He had handed her a street map, the kind that had to be unfolded. If he didn't know the way, why hadn't he got a proper book? This was all crumpled and——

'Look out!'

'Sorry,' he mumbled as he swerved to avoid an oncoming lorry. 'Keep forgetting. Left side, left side. Keep telling me, will you?'

She glanced over at the clean-cut lines of his profile. This was going to be a disastrous ride. Not only did he not know the way, he drove on the wrong side of the road. Catherine tightened her seatbelt, wishing the Rolls-Royce had come supplied with a crash helmet. 'It's left at the next roundabout,' she told him.

'The what?'

'The roundabout, coming up after the next crossing.'

Matt kept his eyes on the road. 'Crossing—intersection, OK.' He had slowed the car. 'Now tell me about roundabouts.'

Catherine sighed. 'A circular intersection. You want to turn left at the next one. See, it's coming up ahead.'

A low grumble might have been an affirmative response. He edged carefully to the left of the moving traffic. 'So which one? They're *all* left!'

'Here, this one!'

There was a pause before he answered. They were still circling with the moving cars. 'Sorry, I missed it. How about this one?'

He had headed for a narrow street, and as they

moved sedately along, she struggled to find their location on the map. 'I don't think so. . .'

'Well, I like it. It's straight.' Matt turned to smile at her, but found only a frowning passenger scanning the streets they passed. The dimming light was no help, and he could never find any street signs anyway.

'Ah,' Catherine nodded. Just as she had thought. 'We're going the wrong way.'

'Oh, I don't know.' Matt's smile widened. 'I sort of like this. I'm beginning to get the hang of the old Duchess here——'

'Who?'

'The Duchess—that's what I call her. Proud, very well bred, but responds perfectly when you know how to treat her.'

Catherine said, 'Well, if you and your duchess ever want to get home some time before next Friday, you'd better get her going in the right direction.' She motioned to an empty car park coming up.

'Oh, all right. Come on then, madam, let's do what the boss says.' With a smooth motion he turned the wheel, and the car responded immediately.

'Left! LEFT!' Catherine's heart had jumped into her mouth.

With a grunt, Matthew moved into the correct lane and they were returning the way they had come. 'Now for that tricky roundabout. I can see where they get the name for it. Here we go again!'

As Catherine held her breath and pressed her back against the seat, they finally achieved the desired exit, and silence reigned for a few moments until Matt started to mutter to himself. 'Left, left. Remember the left.'

Just as she was beginning to hope they might actually manage an accident-free return to the hospital, she heard a happy sigh and followed his glance ahead of them. They had reached a turning for a major motorway, and he slowed to wait for the traffic lights.

'Now, how do I get on the freeway? Be OK there.'

The dry tickle of anxiety was creeping back into her throat; Catherine could imagine the effect the oversized silver limousine would have on three lanes of speeding motorists. 'I think we'd better. . .' She paused, wondering if the old Duchess even had enough in her to keep up to the minimum speed limit. 'Why don't we just keep to the side streets?'

Matt frowned, ignoring the interested examination from a driver idling beside them. 'Too winding, can't keep the directions straight. Now that. . .' he pointed ahead '. . .goes like an arrow.'

'Well, actually it doesn't.' As usual, he thought he knew everything. Once they got on to that motorway they'd never get off it, and she had visions of them driving around in unending circles with the likely possibility of failing to live to tell the tale. 'It's very simple, really——'

'Right, then, that's it.'

'What?' Her hand tightened on the crumpled map at the cold anger in his voice.

'A man can take only so much. Get out.' Without raising his voice from a normal conversational level, Matt began to unbuckle his seatbelt.

'Out?' Catherine stared at the stern face in disbelief. What had she said to cause such an over-reaction? 'I was only trying to——'

'Out, I said. And hurry up about it.' He turned off the engine and was opening his door, oblivious of smiling onlookers.

She couldn't believe what was happening. He was getting ready to throw her out of the car! 'Here?' She looked around. They were in the middle of a busy intersection.

'You'd better get a move on. You're holding up traffic.' Now he was standing by her door, implacable and immovable.

'Why don't you get back in?' She could hear a few comments beginning to come from the adjacent lane. 'Please?'

'No. Out with you!' One large hand reached in and flipped open her seatbelt.

As she stumbled out on to the road, Catherine found herself several feet lower, and the reaction of their audience became louder.

'Bit of a barney, then, mate?'

'Don't you mind 'im, girlie. 'Op over 'ere. Wherever you want, eh?'

Now she had to look up at the face reflected in the amber glow from the street lights. He was looking solemn, and she felt a tiny stab of fear. Would he really leave her here in the middle of nowhere? 'But the lights, they're turning green!' she cried.

Reaching to wrench the map from her hands, Matt asked, 'Have you got a licence?'

'Yes, but ——'

'No buts.' He was sliding into the passenger seat. 'You drive.'

Catherine stood irresolutely on the white line that had suddenly filled her vision. How could she walk home from here? A burst of ribald laughter from the lorry behind them decided her, and she hurried around to climb up into the driver's seat, slamming the door behind her.

'I can't do this.' She turned on him. 'You'd need an HGV licence for this tank!'

Matt was settling himself comfortably. 'Since I don't know what that is, no comment. As you so rightly observed, the light is green. Shall we go?'

As she looked frantically for a gear shift, he pointed, adding. 'All automatic, the only one they had.'

Taking a deep breath and sending up a mute prayer to the gods who watched over damsels in distress, at least those in the company of arrogant self-opinionated and bossy males, Catherine turned the ignition key and eased the car forward across the lights and on to a safe verge, where she managed to stop.

'At least let me try and find out where we are!' She made a grab for the map and was surprised when he made no objection, merely stretching his long legs and languidly handing it over without comment. As she peered at the squiggly lines, his quick flick of a hidden overhead light was a surprise but not much help. She looked up at the traffic now streaming past them, and a bulky familiar shape gave her an idea.

There was only one way to get herself safely home in one piece, and there was nowhere else she wanted to be at this very instant — away from unpredictable men in too-large automobiles. She examined the instrument panel; the old Duchess might lack all the chrome of the modern age, but she seemed to have the essentials.

A push of a button brought on the headlight beams, and Catherine fastened her seatbelt. This might not be so bad after all. Concentrating on the feel of the controls, she joined the moving cars while searching for the first turning. This was accomplished with surprising ease, and she surreptitiously loosened her coat buttons to free her legs and get more comfortable.

It was impossible not to sense the hidden power in the large Rolls-Royce, and Catherine smiled to herself, as she took another corner on a smooth turn.

'Now where are we going?' Matt asked in a tone of polite interest.

'Home.' She was looking for a particular street

name, and spoke more confidently as she saw it. 'Straight home.'

'Looks like the scenic route.' He was watching the darkened streets slide past the window.

Seeing what she was looking for looming ahead, she allowed a tinge of sarcasm to slip through. 'It's the bus route.'

Matt shot a quick smile across at her and straightened himself up into a position that necessitated the spread of a long arm across the back of the seats. 'Good. I get to look at the scenery. A guided tour would be appreciated.'

'No way!' Catherine was beginning to enjoy herself; it was fun to be sitting so high above the road, and this car was a dream to drive. She would be completely at ease if only she didn't have someone intent on looking at her side all the time. She wished he'd stare out of his own window. 'Why didn't you hire an American car?' she added.

Matt's gaze did not waver. He liked what he was looking at. 'They didn't have any. Besides, I took a fancy to the Duchess. Seems she's taken a fancy to you as well.'

Ignoring his comment, she eased up to close behind the bus she was following. At this rate they'd have to slow at every local stop, but she couldn't risk losing her trusted pilot, even if he was at the wheel of a green and yellow striped double-decker bus.

'I always wanted a chauffeur.' Matt was continuing to talk casually as his hands absently stroked the leather-edged seat behind her shoulder. 'You know, you'd look good in a peaked cap, even if it was crooked.'

'Would you kindly shut up? We'll end up in a ditch if you don't stop distracting me!'

'Mmm.' He did not sound the least bit apologetic

and his hand continued silent movements beside her ear. 'A distraction, am I?'

Catherine tightened her hands on the wheel. If only she had thought of trying to find the familiar bus before now, she could have accepted his threat to throw her out on the roadside and marched off defiantly into the sunset. Too late now. Impatiently she jiggled her foot on the accelerator. 'Come on, come on!' she urged the unseen bus driver. The Rolls let out a small unhappy hiccough at her misuse of the pedal just as the grinding gears ahead of them signalled forward movement. 'It's about time!'

Matt's hand had moved closer to her neck and was touching the tip of a shimmering gold drop almost hidden by a wayward curl. 'Beautiful. Shines like precious treasure.'

'Thank you.' Catherine tried to angle her head away from his fingers, but had to straighten up to swing out behind the lorry obstructing her view of the bus. She spoke with a touch of asperity, wishing he would keep his hands to himself. 'They were a recent gift.'

'Ah. Someone knows what suits you.'

'Yes, he does. Better than anyone else in the world.'

Matt's hand stilled. Her expression had softened into a tenderness that was reflected in her voice. So there was a special someone, a man, in her life. There would have to be, wouldn't there? A woman with such vibrancy simmering under the cool surface could hardly be alone. Just as a quick stab of envy for the fortunate unknown person who could bring the gentle smile to those kissable lips pricked at the edge of his mind he had a cheering thought.

She could have a doting father. 'A family birthday present?' he asked.

Catherine had drawn up behind the bus again idling for passengers and she turned, speaking brusquely.

'How can I drive with you chattering away like a demented monkey and crawling all over?' She flicked at his hand near her shoulder. She knew she was really angry at herself for speaking about Mark. Those feelings were private and would never be understood by strangers, especially pushy people who were persistently rude.

'You're about to miss your bus.'

Muttering a mild oath under her breath, Catherine returned her attention to the road. Surely it couldn't be much further; the spacious interior of the car was beginning to feel much too warm and close. Just as she was beginning to wonder if the bus driver might develop an understandable curiosity about the ancient Rolls steadily trailing him, she spotted a familiar landmark and swung away down a side-street.

'Now where are we?' Matt sounded thoughtful, as if he was not talking about the local geography.

'I know where I'm going,' she assured him.

'That's good, because I'm not so sure where *I'm* going.'

Well, that's your problem, Catherine answered silently. Soon she would be safely home and could leave the Duchess and her temporary custodian to their own devices. She eased around the final corner, hoping desperately that there was no one about to observe their arrival.

'This is where I live,' she said.

'Here?' He sounded disbelieving.

Switching off the ignition with a firm twist, Catherine began to fumble with the belt clasp.

Matt was craning his neck to see beyond her bent head. 'Looks like a fortress. What *is* this?'

'It's the staff residence.' At last she was free and reached for the door-handle. 'And I like it.'

'Really?' Muttering something about fair maidens in

lofty towers, he slid out easily from the passenger side. 'Does this forbidding exterior hold hidden delights that others can only wonder at?'

'I have no idea.' Catherine struggled to get her long legs over the high door frame, making a grab for her concealing coat at the same time as pushing at the heavy door.

Not fast enough. Matt sidestepped her forceful shove and reached for her hands. In an instinctive movement to evade his grasp, Catherine stumbled and caught her low heel on the metal ridge. Immediately her waist was encircled by exceedingly muscular arms.

'What —— ?' she began.

No further words were possible as a warm mouth covered hers and all rational thought fled into the night. His kiss was slow and thoughtful, gently massaging her lips in a tentative exploration that sent tingling waves of sensation down to the tips of her toes.

For an instant she knew she was responding to the delicious warmth of the hands that were spreading liquid fire down her spine. It would be too easy to drown in the tantalising whirlpool of feelings blurring her brain.

As his mouth moved to touch her cheek, Catherine took a deep breath, pushed back against the open door and swung with all her might towards his head.

Too late. With a swiftness born of experience he ducked, and the blow merely grazed his nose, eliciting only a surprised, 'Humph!'

Furious that she had been goaded into such behaviour, Catherine also felt humiliated. Somehow she had been bested in a conflict she couldn't stop to identify. His bulk was blocking her escape, and she tried to shove past. As his hand was rubbing his nose, she managed to squeeze against his upraised elbow.

'Temper, temper! But I *do* like those little green glints.' Matt's voice was gruffly nasal.

'You. . .you *toad*!' Any words she tried to think up were inadequate to describe this man. Everything was a jumble of heat and fury, and her head was swimming in circles. 'Just take your stupid Duchess and disappear!'

Matt leaned against the open door, watching her scrabble inside her bag. 'Methinks the lady was not entirely immune.' He reached out as if to touch her arm, but a rapid movement made him withdraw and he hunched his shoulder protectively. 'Enough, my beautiful Catherine. This protuberance has suffered enough.'

'I hope it falls off!' With this final, and futile, riposte Catherine gathered her coat around her and attempted a dignified retreat up the steps. Her feet were none too steady and her hands were shaking, but with a concentrated effort she managed to fit the key into the lock and swing the door behind her with a most satisfactory clang.

Waiting until she was safely inside the building, Matt stood motionless, watching until a new light appeared in an upstairs window. Finally he slid back behind the wheel and patted the gleaming dashboard before shifting into gear. 'First play brought out a strong defence, but we can always change the game plan, eh, old girl?' He was whistling softly between his teeth as he drove off into the darkness, a rhythm reminiscent of chanting support for the home team suffering a temporary setback on the scoreboard.

'He's a heaven-sent miracle, that man!'

Catherine offered no response as she watched the unit sister busily emptying a shelf in the medicine refrigerator.

'What's happening?' she asked.

'The antibiotics will have to go into the kitchen fridge. They should be safe enough there, unless Mrs Petrussi mistakes them for a new type of pepperpot.' The greying head bobbed up from a bottom shelf under the unit sink where extra boxes were stored. Sister was smiling happily. 'Just what we've been praying for — the EPO the pharmacy said that they couldn't get.'

Helping to stack the few trays of dislodged antibiotics, Catherine watched the senior nurse began to slice through the plastic tapes on the slim box on the counter. As the precious vials appeared, the sister continued to talk animatedly. 'He says he can get enough for everyone but needs named patients, so we're having a team meeting after tea to go over all the notes. He says he can get a course for forty patients, if we need it.'

'Who?' Already knowing the answer, Catherine asked the question automatically. Only one person could have done this; it had been his first "problem". But enough for all the patients? What would he have done if she had told him they had eighty patients? Probably get enough for a hundred.

'Matthew Dunnegan, that's who, bless him.'

'But how?' Catherine persisted.

The sister shrugged. 'I don't know, but it's here, and that's all I care about. The first patient will be Jackie and you know what it will mean for her.'

Catherine nodded. They weren't supposed to ask about how the new surgeon worked his magic, just accept with unquestioning gratitude. Well, she didn't trust him. Not one inch. What had he done to get such an apparently inexhaustible supply of a very expensive drug? She brought her attention back; Eileen Smythe was still talking.

'And she's going on haemodialysis.'

'What? Jackie?'

'Yes, she's being prepared for transplant.'

'But she's been doing so well on peritoneal. I thought——' Catherine began.

The unit sister had finished packing away the precious drug and turned after locking the medicine refrigerator. 'Yes, I know, Catherine. You've taught her and her mother well, but she's not fit enough yet for a transplant.'

'But——' How could she say that it was unlikely anyone new, however ingenious, could find a donor when everyone else had failed for the past two years?

'The sooner the better—you know that. She'll need at least a momth on haemo before her urea and creatinine will be controlled enough. Can you start preparing her tomorrow, please?'

'Of course, Sister.' Immediately Catherine began to plan her teaching, but there was one niggling and essential question to be answered. 'What access is planned?'

'He's going to do a subclavian, some time this week. Our Mr Dunnegan certainly doesn't believe in wasting time!'

Catherine knew she could vouch for the truth of that statement. The days following Matt's overwhelming effect on her stability had brought a more balanced consideration of Sunday's events. It must be that American men behaved like that—rushing their fences. At any rate, she hadn't seen him since, and the memory of that burning kiss was beginning to lose the edge of anger that he could have taken her for granted. It had been a goodnight kiss, nothing more. More forceful than most, but it obviously hadn't meant anything to him, since he seemed to have disappeared from the face of the earth. So much the better. She could concentrate on more important things.

'Hello, Catherine. Did you hear about the EPO?' Emily had brought in a lunch tray where Catherine was stacking antibiotics into the fridge.

'Mmm, it'll help Jackie.' She finished her chore and turned. 'He's planning haemo for her with a subclavian. Why would he put a child through all the trauma of a general anaesthetic? She could have an arterial fistula without all that.'

'Maybe. Seems to me he's a man who knows what he's doing.' Emily eyed her friend cautiously. Catherine had been remarkably uncommunicative about her ride home with the handsome surgeon. 'Seen him lately?'

'No. Whose tray is that?'

'Mrs Murphy's.' Emily accepted defeat. 'She's really doing well on the new machine. Her weight is staying down and she's much less wobbly after treatments. Says she can even attack the laundry when she gets home!'

Wondering if she could schedule Jackie for time on the new machine, Catherine missed what Emily was saying. 'Sorry. . .?'

'I said, Matt's even got Josh on Cloud Nine. Apparently he's going to buy a lot of the computer gizmos the company sells, and Josh says he might get a promotion out of it.'

'That's great, Em!' Catherine smiled and began to push the massive food trolley out into the corridor to be collected by the kitchen porter. She didn't want to discuss Matthew Dunnegan with anyone, especially since he seemed to be weaving his charming tentacles around everyone she knew. 'I'll disconnect Mrs Murphy. See you later.'

Mrs Murphy's obvious delight with her own progress reinforced Catherine's determination to book the newest machine for Jackie.

'See, it's almost my dry weight!' she exclaimed.

Watching over the patient's shoulder as Mrs Murphy expertly slid the weights on the floor scales, Catherine agreed. 'It's much better, and staying down too.'

The broad face was wreathed in a proud smile. 'And I don't have to watch all the cups of tea so much.'

'Oh, yes, you do!' Catherine laughed. 'Just because this machine works better, it doesn't mean you can be lazy!'

Seeing that Mrs Murphy was indeed feeling well and needed little help in dressing to go home, Catherine made her way to Jackie's bed. The little girl was sitting up, waiting to be disconnected from the peritoneal dialysis bags hanging above her head.

'Mummy says I'm going to use a big machine, Nurse. Is that true? Am I going to get a new kidney? Is that why? Is it?'

'I don't know.' Catherine had to be truthful with the child who trusted her. She would never make promises she couldn't keep, not like some other people she could think of. 'First we'll have to put the catheter in the right place for the machine to work, and it's different from the one in your tummy now.'

The little girl's eyes widened. 'Where does it go? In my arm, like Mrs Murphy?'

Hearing her name, the woman paused in her dressing and waved cheerily. Jackie continued, 'I'd like that, then I won't have all those bags on the pole.'

'No more poles.' Catherine spied the well-loved panda half hidden in the bedclothes. 'Here, I'll show you on Solomon.' There was no time like the present to begin teaching. 'Just about here, near the shoulder.'

'Can he have one too?' asked Jackie.

'Of course. We'll do that for practice tomorrow. We'll give him a little slit to connect the vein just under here,' Catherine pressed lightly under Jackie's collarbone, 'so the blood can be washed clean.'

'No more sloshing around in my tummy?'

Catherine smiled and nodded. 'No more sloshing.'

'Does it hurt?' The big blue eyes were anxious. 'Solomon doesn't like being hurt.'

Catherine held the panda's paws gently. 'Of course he doesn't.' She gave Jackie a hug. 'Once the tube is in place, nice and secure, he'll forget it's even there. But I think that's enough for today. Your mummy will be here to collect you, and we'd better get you ready.'

As she busied herself with familiar routines after Jackie's departure, Catherine was satisfied with her first efforts at introducing the child to a new treatment. If only certain individuals didn't want to rush everything, she'd be able to do the job properly. At the end of the afternoon shift, she checked the ward diary, and was not surprised to find the child's first haemodialysis scheduled for Friday. That gave her only one day for teaching, not enough time.

She was frowning as she pencilled in '?Cobe' next to Jackie's name. At least she might have the best machine. She hoped the impatient surgeon had booked his own theatre time; if not, that was his problem.

'Catherine, can you take this EPO patient list to Mr Dunnegan's office on your way out?'

'Of course, Sister.' She wouldn't be off duty until seven o'clock and all the offices would be empty.

'If we send it by internal post it won't get there for another day. Oh, and there's this. It's not for any of our patients, so it must have come here by mistake.'

Catherine looked at the personal prescription sheet attached to the white pharmacy bag. Levodopa. That was strange. There were no renal patients needing this drug, but the signature was clearly M. Dunnegan. Unusually for a doctor, his writing was neat and legible.

It was really none of her concern, and she tucked the list and prescription into her holdall. A detour on her way to the tennis practice with Danny was a nuisance, but if Mr Dunnegan wanted his precious list then she'd make sure he had no cause to complain about the efficiency of the renal unit staff.

CHAPTER FIVE

As she passed the closed door of the professor's office in the main hospital building, Catherine was relieved that there was no one around to see her wandering around in her blue tracksuit through the silent corridors. She must look like a brightly dressed burglar with her sports bag bulging, showing the end of a metal racquet handle.

Not that there's much to steal here without a forklift trolley to carry it away, she thought as she searched for names on the doors nearly hidden behind vivid representations of kidney diseases on the research posters lining the walls.

She ignored the mottled ultrasound photographs surrounded by technical graphs and drawings that to her eyes were remote from real patients. People who chose to spend their medical lives surrounded by the mechanical paraphernalia of research instead of living, breathing people would always be a mystery to her.

A light under one door shot a sharp beacon across the floor. It seemed there was one person still at work. Her heart sank. Who else would it be but one over-enthusiastic surgeon? She tapped at the door.

'Come.'

The doorknob resisted Catherine's attempt to turn it, and she knocked more loudly. Suddenly the door swung open, and the sudden light made her blink.

'Sorry, I forgot to undo —— Well, hello!'

Looking up into the grey eyes smiling at her with genuine warmth, Catherine was suddenly aware of how tired he looked. There were dark rings under his eyes, accentuating the strong cheekbones, but that smile still had the effect of causing little skips in her pulse rate. He was eyeing her bag with a raised eyebrow.

'Have you sought me out in my den to deliver another deadly blow?' Matt rubbed the side of his nose with one long finger.

Catherine swung her bag behind her back, hiding the protruding handle. 'Of course not! I brought these — the EPO list you asked for. And this.' She watched his face as she held out the pharmacy prescription.

'Thanks.' His face was inscrutable as he took the small white paper bag and shoved it into his jacket pocket, slung over a chair. He kept the list to examine as he moved nearer a long narrow desk. 'Only twenty-two? Well, that will have to do.'

Knowing she should leave, having fulfilled her errand, Catherine hesitated. Her curiosity was aroused. Why did he write a prescription for Levodopa? In his rolled-up shirtsleeves, there was no evidence of any neurological disability to indicate a need for such a drug; on the contrary, he looked exceedingly strong and steady. Nothing short of a seismic eruption would shake Matt Dunnegan's equilibrium. And there was something else.

'How can you —— ?' she began.

'How can I what?' He spoke quickly, looking at her sharply through half-lidded eyes, his expression guarded.

'Get that much EPO. It costs the earth!'

Matt let out a short laugh, with a hint of relief. 'I got somebody else to pay for it.' He waved at a neat pile of correspondence. 'Our chat in the bar gave me the idea of using what you lot call the old boys' network. Thanks to a fax machine.'

Catherine looked where he was pointing towards a cream-coloured box lined up beside two tidy stacks of paperwork. He was obviously careful about where he put things; everything according to his plans. For some reason, she felt nettled.

'So who's paying?' she asked.

'You really don't trust me, do you?' Matt brushed the list of names close to her uplifted chin. 'Nothing illegal, just a little indirect, shall we say. An American drug company has a branch over here, and they agreed to continue the research grant they gave me in Toronto. A different area of study, but the last one was useful, so they went along with another. This time it's the demonstrable benefit of EPO for transplant patients' long-term outcome. No problem showing that.'

'But they're not all getting transplants,' she said, flicking at the paper in front of her face.

'There, those green glints are starting again. Lovely!' He grinned at her. 'You really shouldn't wear blue — clashes with all that fire you're directing at me.' He lifted his hands in mock penitence. 'If you don't tell the moneybag people, I won't. The patients will get their anaemia treated, and who knows, I might find a few more donors. That's the next problem.'

Catherine edged away from the broad-shouldered man and his irritating grin.

He looked at her enquiringly. 'Have you had supper? I'm starving!'

She could well believe that; the man did nothing but eat at every opportunity. 'I ate on the unit,' she told him.

'That figures.' He inclined his head towards his desk. 'Do you know anything about computers?'

'Not really.' Catherine tried to move backwards, but her feet weren't obeying. 'I thought Josh had been here.'

'Oh, yeah, but that's not what I need. Don't you

have a terminal on the dialysis unit? For lab results, or something?'

'Yes, but——'

'Good. What's your code?'

She couldn't think of any reason why he shouldn't know it; they were members of the same team, after all. 'DIALAB. They change it every three months.'

'Can you show me?'

Shrugging off her heavy bag, Catherine moved towards the unlit computer screen. 'I suppose so.' As she switched on the equipment she could see him pulling out a little red notebook and scribbling in it. Just like an address book with girlfriends' phone numbers, she thought. Except his is for computer passwords. Not much difference, really. 'There, that's what we get. Blood chemistry with this,' she punched a key while he watched over her shoulder, 'urinalysis with this, and if you want things like histology or microbiology you need numbered digits instead of letters.'

'Can you get Jackie's tissue-typing?'

His warm breath on her neck was causing the tingling ripples to creep down her spine again, and she tried to ease away from the arms now encircling her chair. 'No, we don't need it.'

'So, how do I get the last three months' creatinine clearances?'

Keeping her concentration on the green flickering digits on the screen in front of them, Catherine pulled up the menu for chemical pathology and punched in Jackie's hospital number that she knew by heart. The values were swinging wildly beyond normal, even she could see that.

Before she could react, Matt's hands came across hers on the keyboard, and the giddy sensation of being engulfed in warm muskiness drew a sharp intake of breath. She tried to still her trembling fingers. 'Just what are you planning on trying?' she asked curiously.

A deep rumble of laughter reverberated against her back, and she found she was leaning against a soft shirt; there didn't seem to be anywhere else to go. 'Checking on Jackie's results. Now, let's take a look.'

As he shifted his position to manipulate the keys, Catherine edged out from under his arm, but she was still pinned next to the desk. Those creatinine clearances results were not good.

'Do you really think haemodialysis will help?' she asked.

'Not for long.' Matt moved over to a machine beside the terminal. 'Now, how do I do this?' He punched a button and the machine began to clatter before rolling out a printed perforated sheet. He shook his head as he scanned the long lines of numbers.

'No one expects her to get a transplant, you know,' said Catherine.

'So it seems.' Matt's voice was quiet as he continued to stare at the figures on the print-out, as if he could change them with the force of his glare.

Catherine persisted. 'The Prof says her blood type is too difficult, AB negative, I think, let alone all the rest of the factors.' She felt his eyes on her and was surprised by the anger obvious in the fixed set of his jaw. The soft grey in his tired eyes had turned to a dark coolness that made her skin prickle.

'I'm not concerned with what the professor says. I need information to get what I want, and by God, I'll get it!'

He was insulting the one person they all depended on for their very existence. Who was he to set himself above the head of the unit? 'You have no right — !' she began.

'No right to what?' Now his eyes were boring into

hers. 'No right to question an assumption that a child will never get a transplant? So maybe there *are* four thousand patients waiting for donors, but if no one even tries to get one little girl an even chance with the others, whose right is that? I'll bet her name isn't even on the list!'

Catherine opened her mouth to deny this, even though she didn't know whether Jackie was on any list, but he was not to be stopped.

'You think she has to survive for whatever time she might have for a limited and uncomfortable life on your precious machines, tended by dedicated nurses such as yourself?'

'You have no right to criticise the professor!' Catherine ignored his implied slur on her own work. He couldn't understand what it meant to care for people who became as close as family, over months and years of treatment.

Matt slowly folded the sheet in his hands and sighed. 'Sometimes things change, my sweet Nurse Catherine. Sometimes ideas can be changed when seen in a new light.'

'And you're the new light, I suppose. Come to show us the error of our ways and change the world.' She was reaching for her bag.

Matt smiled briefly. 'Hardly. But the child needs someone on her side, and I don't give up easily.'

That fleeting smile brought an easing of the frown creasing his broad forehead, and Catherine decided it was definitely time to get out of this office. She'd forgotten all about the waiting Danny. 'I'm leaving. I'm already late.'

Matt reached for his jacket. 'Great. You off to the Rec Club?'

For such a large man he did move quickly, and before she could reach the door he had shrugged into his coat and was waiting with an arm outstretched for her to lead the way.

'I could use some of Carlos's tortillas. I'll take that.'

He had her holdall out of her grasp with equal swiftness, and Catherine decided there was no sense in arguing with such an overbearing man. She stepped briskly into the darkened corridor, and wasn't surprised when he easily kept step with her. Obviously there was no shaking him off, but she didn't have to answer his casual comments on the lovely night and the clarity of the moonlight.

As she expected, Danny was waiting, and was looking distinctly put out.

'It's about time, Cath. We're losing our court time.' His eyes fell on the tall man holding her bag. 'Oh, sorry.'

As she hurriedly introduced them Catherine noted the tight smile on Danny's face contrasting with the wide friendly grin of the doctor pumping his hand.

'Hi. Glad to know you. You work at the hospital?'

Danny had recognised the doctor's name, but couldn't immediately think why. 'In the path labs. You play?' He nodded at Catherine's bag.

'Tennis? No way!' Matt laughed. 'Just over here for a bite to eat. The bar still open?'

'Sure, till eleven.' Danny looked relieved. 'You coming, Cath?'

Regaining possession of her belongings, Catherine nodded. She almost bumped into the doctor, who had made a swift U-turn.

'By the way, Danny,' Matt asked casually,' do you do antigen testing? T and B cells?'

The question reminded Danny where he had seen this doctor's name before—on a request for a few hundred tissue-typing results. 'We can do, but your own renal labs do most of it. We only do the leukaemics and bone marrow transplant stuff.'

'Right—thanks. Have a good game.' With a smile and what might have been construed as a wink at Catherine, Matthew Dunnegan finally made his way towards the bar and food.

Catherine didn't wait to see if Danny was following as she headed for the locker-rooms. She was in a hurry to bash something—hard!

It was Danny who felt the results of her explosion of energy as he dodged the first fierce serve she sent shooting across the net.

'Hey, Cath! Give us a break!' He ran to reach the sliced curve directed at his backhand and held up a hand. 'You don't need the practice serving. It's me that needs that.'

'A couple more, then I'll quit.' She tossed the ball high and stretched on her toes to throw all her weight behind the racquet. It was a glorious feeling to use every ounce of power she could muster and hear the satisfying thunk as she caught the ball in the dead centre of the webbing. A wonderful feeling.

Danny had given up and waited, bouncing balls on the ground. There was no sense in even trying to volley such stinging serves, and after a moment of peace he looked up, hoping she was ready for more deliberate practice. Now she was staring at the sidelines. 'Hey, Cath?' he called.

Catherine was glaring at the observer, who was sitting, placidly munching an oversized stuffed roll, on a chair tipped against the wall. Why would Matt Dunnegan bother watching a game he had implied he knew nothing about?

'Come on, Cath, let's do some net work.' Danny didn't care who watched, so long as they got on with it.

Obediently, Catherine moved to the net and nodded.

She would show someone that she could play at least one game better than he could!

As her partner lobbed and volleyed in every direction, she concentrated on defence. Nothing passed her, and Catherine had never felt her senses so alive. Her feet moved as if on cushions of speeding air and her eyes missed nothing. Danny's attacks were futile; she countered them all and began to smash his too-easy lobs until he gave up.

'Enough, Cath. Let's switch courts.'

Glancing sideways, Catherine saw that their audience of one had finished his snack and was examining the tournament rota of players on the bulletin board. Before she looked away he stepped back, turned to nod and wave at her before disappearing through the swing doors.

'Seen enough, have you?' she muttered. Now it was her turn to receive Danny's serve, but her attention was wandering, and she contented herself with collecting the balls and throwing them back. There were more important things to worry about than a staff tennis tournament.

Some people didn't play by the rules, even if they knew what they were. Matthew Dunnegan had already altered the treatment of many of their long-term patients and was obviously planning more transformations in their lives. She would have to be ready for him, preferably one step ahead of a mind that operated on permanent overdrive. He was the problem, a man who couldn't leave well enough alone but had to meddle and interfere where he wasn't needed. No trespassers allowed—that was it. She would have to watch his every move and keep their world safe from his intrusion.

* * *

'What does Prof say about the EPO?' Catherine asked the ward sister on Friday morning. The Thursday ward round had been cancelled when she might have had a chance to check with the head of the unit.

'He's countersigned all the prescriptions, so he must be as pleased as the rest of us,' said Sister.

'Did he cancel yesterday's round?' Catherine asked as she double-checked the medicine trolley before locking it away. The nursing staff did not expect doctors to appear regularly as they did on in-patient wards and were quite accustomed to summon medical staff only in emergencies, but for once Catherine would have been vaguely relieved to have seen the professor's reaction for herself.

'Probably had something else on and there's nothing urgent here.' Eileen Smythe was straightening the bulging chart rack. 'I notice you booked the new machine for Jackie today. That was a good idea. Did you see her haemoglobin is already higher? Was she NPO this morning?'

Before Catherine could answer in the affirmative, a familiar voice intervened. 'Not necessary, Sister. A local anaesthetic will suffice.'

Both nurses whirled around. Neither had expected to see him on the unit, but it was Eileen Smythe who recovered first.

'Good morning, Doctor. We didn't expect to see ——'

'Now, Smitty, I've told you the name is Matt.'

To Catherine's amusement, a flush of pleasure appeared on the unit sister's cheeks. 'Now, Mr Dunnegan, none of that, if you please. What is it you're looking for?'

The dark head had leaned between the two women to read the sheet held in the sister's hand. 'Higher haemoglobin already? Good. Now where's that terminal I've heard about?'

'It's out by the reception desk,' Catherine answered smoothly.

Matt nodded cheerfully and disappeared to the outer office area. In a few minutes he called out, 'Found it!'

'Better follow him.' The unit sister had replaced the blood result form in Jackie's notes. 'I'll finish the meds. You see what he's after.'

Hearing the note of fond resignation in Eileen's voice, Catherine knew Matthew Dunnegan had made another conquest; now he had their head nurse eating out of his hand. She could only wonder who would be next.

'What are you doing?' she asked. He had punched up a program she had never seen before and was running one finger along a row of data.

'Transplant typing for potential donors.'

No one on their unit had ever used such information, that she knew. 'How did you get that?' she demanded.

Matt skewed his tall frame around on the stool and winked at her. 'You just need the right password. Then it's "Open sesame" and all will be revealed!'

Ignoring the wink that seemed to have a conspiratorial message, Catherine noticed the open pages of the small red notebook. So he had been busy collecting computer codes. She wondered who had been inveigled into providing access to what must be restricted information.

'Do you want to see Jackie? She's not due in for another half-hour.'

Matt finished examining several pages of linear numbers and then turned off the terminal. 'No. First I need to see the equipment you've got. It might be a bit different from what I'm used to.'

Just as the message that he was going to do the

procedure on the unit penetrated Catherine's brain, her eyes were drawn to a long cellophane-wrapped tube sticking out of his top pocket.

He patted the pocket she was staring at. 'Brought my own paediatric catheter. It lasts up to four weeks — that should be long enough.'

Long enough for what? she wanted to ask. 'You're not doing a GA in theatre?' she queried.

'No. Too scary for the young 'uns.' Again he was waiting for her to lead the way, and Catherine hurried towards the equipment stores, thankful for their daily checks on the trays and hoping that everything was as it should be. Apparently it wasn't.

'Sorry. I'm going to need undiluted heparin, please.' Matt sounded apologetic as he poked under the top cover of the subclavian tray. 'Without sterile saline, nought point five mls with five thousand units. Other stuff prolongs anti-coagulation times a bit too much.'

'Yes, Doctor.' Something else new. Well, if that was what he wanted, that was what she would get. A quick check of the ward medicine cupboard produced the desired drug, and she added the narrow-necked vial to the range of local anaesthetics already prepared.

'Is there anything else you need, Doctor?'

A wicked gleam lit up Matt's face as Catherine asked her dutiful and professional question. 'Well, now that you mention it——'

'Hi, you two. Jackie and her mum have just come in.' Emily poked her head around the open door. She grinned brightly. 'Hope I didn't interrupt anything, but I thought you might like to know.'

'Thanks, Em,' Catherine answered. Whatever Matt had been about to mention, she was sure it wasn't surgical equipment. 'I'll go and get Jackie ready.'

'Right. Be with you in about fifteen minutes, after I have a word with Mum.' Matt had pulled out a surgical gown and mask packet and was riffling through the sterile glove supply. 'Where are the seven and a halfs?'

'On the tray.' Catherine didn't mention that she had surreptitiously slid several different sizes on under the covering linen. His hands must be slim if he wanted the smaller size for the skin-tight coverings. She didn't wait to see his reaction but concentrated on the task ahead. It wouldn't be easy, no matter how light-hearted the surgeon might be about his work.

She found the little girl already sitting up in bed, dressed in a new nightie, clasping her panda for comfort. The stuffed animal was sprouting a striped plastic straw anchored with a tight dressing from his furry shoulder.

'Dr Matt? Is he coming?' asked the little girl.

'He won't be long, Jackie. He's talking with your mum,' Catherine answered. 'Now we have to raise you up.' As she spoke, she pushed the electronic button and the child smiled with delight. Catherine found it hard to gauge the correct height for Matt Dunnegan, he was so tall. She remembered that his chin was just about the level of her nose, and had that odd little cleft. . . She banished the unexpected image. Surely this would be high enough. Any more and the child would be swinging from the ceiling fan. 'There. How's that?'

'It's nice up here. I can see everybody. Now I lie down, like this.'

Catherine smiled as Jackie flattened herself on the bed. At least she remembered everything she had been told. She moved to draw the cream curtains around the bed, glancing briefly at Mrs Murphy in the next bed. For once, the voluble lady was fast asleep.

Jackie was watching her every move. 'Do you think Dr Matt has spoken to St Nick yet?' she asked. 'About my kidney, I mean.'

'I don't know, Jackie. You'll have to ask *him* that,' Catherine answered gently. This child's excellent memory might become an intractable problem, but Matt Dunnegan could get himself out of his own careless promises. 'Now, you need a pad under your neck, remember?'

'Can Solomon have one too?'

As she settled the little panda, Catherine just had the over-bed table in position as Matt returned with the covered sterile tray. She was mildly surprised to see him doing his own fetching and carrying, but then she would expect him to do things differently. She looked behind him.

'Is Mrs Lasaria coming?' she asked.

Jackie answered promptly. 'Mummy hates needles, but they don't bother me. Hello, Dr Matt.'

'Good morning, Miss Jacqueline.' Matt spoke with a soft drawl, but his face was serious as he turned to scrub at the bedside sink. Catherine was ready with a sterile gown, and he smoothly slid on a pair of paper-thin rubber gloves as she fastened his face mask.

He spoke through the fine gauze. 'Your mum will be along later. All ready?'

Jackie's face had become less cheerful. 'I. . . I think so. Solomon already has his tube in. See?'

'Yes, I do see.' His voice was quiet as his eyes flicked over the red and white straw poking out of the real double-flapped tape. 'Looks most professional, too. Shall we see if we can do as well?'

Matt glanced at Catherine, nodded briefly and began to draw up the small syringe of local anaesthetic.

Understanding that he had withdrawn into clinical concentration, Catherine smothered the tiny glow of pleasure at his compliment. Little did he know how many times Solomon had been subjected to an imitation of what he was preparing to do now, but without any of the hazards Catherine knew lay ahead.

She gently moved Jackie's head to the side, away from the doctor, leaving the neck region clear. Matt swiftly washed the area, and the sweet pungent smell of povidone iodine filled the air before he expertly draped the sterile towels over the small chest.

In Theatre, others would do that for him, Catherine knew as she began to murmur comfort to the little girl. Matt looked as if he was capable of dealing with any situation as he found it. She hoped that was true this time.

'Here comes the bee-sting!'

Catherine grasped Jackie's hand, and just as he spoke, Matt flicked the fine needle under the skin. The child did not even flinch as the liquid was eased into the insertion site.

As he picked up a haemostat, Catherine realised he was going to make a tunnel from an opening under the clavicle. This was a different procedure from the one taught by the professor, and she hoped the catheter was short enough. Then she remembered; he had brought his own. Already he had the needle inserted into the vein, was drawing back blood and preparing the guide wire.

Catherine held her breath. This was the dangerous part. She kept her eyes glued on the deliberately slow movement of the catheter guide deep into the subclavian vein.

Suddenly a penetrating buzz shattered her rapt attention, and Matt's hand froze into immobility.

CHAPTER SIX

'OI! IT's only me! I think I'm done, Nurse.'

It was Mrs Murphy's loud voice coming seconds after the buzz that drew a long breath from Catherine. She met Matt's eyes and gave a little nod as she saw his eyes look up at the ceiling briefly in exasperation.

'It's OK, I've got it.' Emily's calm words were heard above the scurry of soft-soled shoes and the rustle of a uniform skirt.

Matt hesitated, then continued to direct the wire, moving it a fraction before reaching for the catheter. Catherine had been ahead of him and had the stripped end waiting for his searching hand. Without lifting his eyes from the wire, he grunted what might have been thanks before sliding it smoothly over the wire.

As he carefully removed the guide and the catheter was in place, Catherine felt her shoulders relax. It was done; the rest was routine.

'Now you have your tube just like Solomon,' she told Jackie. The catheter had been eased through the subcutaneous tunnel, and she reached for the dressing pack. A single stitch closed the minute incision site, and she promptly placed an inch of dressing firmly over the opening. 'Now comes the one you like.'

Matt had stood back and removed his mask, but kept his attention on the clamp at the end of the catheter. He nodded with satisfaction as Catherine expertly applied the double-edged dressing. 'We need lock caps and safety tapes as well, for X-ray,' he said.

He was shrugging off his gown, and Catherine adjusted Jackie's nightgown. At least she had been prepared for this; the wheelchair had been ordered. She said to the little girl, 'All finished.'

'Can I see?' As Jackie struggled to sit up, she lowered her chin to her chest. 'Is it as good as Solomon's?'

'Better. Much better.' Matt finally smiled. This child had too much fluid in her tissues; he hoped her weight had been recorded. Haemodialysis should have been started long before this. He felt the tension in his arms ease, but his spine hadn't been troubled. For once, the treatment level had been high enough, and he widened his smile as he watched Catherine tidying up the treatment tray.

Not only a beauty, but competent as well. Nice to work with. It was like having someone read your thoughts before you had them, and it had been a long time since he'd had that feeling. He just hoped she couldn't read all of them quite so clearly.

He turned his attention to his small patient. 'Now for a trip to the movies!'

Jackie squealed with delight as he promptly scooped her up in his arms and made a move towards the door.

'She's too heavy!' Catherine was astonished.

'Nonsense!' Matt paused, smiling with a teasing glint in his eyes. 'Now, if it were you that might be a different matter!'

Ignoring his comment, Catherine pointed to the waiting wheelchair. She knew the child's weight to the nearest decimal point, and she was not light, especially before dialysis.

Matt refused to look at the chair. 'We could use a blanket, though, since this unit is in the back of beyond and we've got a long trek ahead of us. Do you think Mum might like to come with us?'

'Maybe, if there's no needles,' Jackie said doubtfully,

and tightened her arms around this funny doctor's neck.

Keeping her retort unspoken, Catherine attempted to wrap a warm blanket around the little girl, as much as she could get around the muscled arms holding her so easily.

'We'll ask her, and when we come back, Nurse will have a machine waiting for our big moment, and I'll bet it's Mrs Murphy's!'

Unable to resist a smile at his accurate guess, Catherine watched as he strode out of the room, carrying the child as if she weighed nothing. He had been so insistent about that. She frowned briefly. Perhaps he thought the catheter might be jiggled or bounced out of position, and if it had been misplaced. . . She shook her head. He was a good surgeon; she had seen that for herself. This was not a man who made mistakes. He just liked surprising people, and Jackie was obviously enjoying herself enormously.

There was no time to be spent in idle thoughts; she would have to hurry to have everything ready for their return.

'Here, dear, you do the wash-out and I'll make the bed, if you'll get it down again.' Mrs Murphy was now fully dressed and had pulled back the dividing curtain.

Glad of the extra help, Catherine said, 'It was good of you to come in early to free the new machine.'

'Deserves the best, that little girlie.' With the ease of years of practice, the middle-edged patient was stripping the bed. 'Nice to have the energy to do this again.'

'And I'm grateful for your help. Here, I'll do that.' Taking the used instrument tray back to the utility-room, Catherine again reflected on the importance of support from the patients. They knew as much about their illnesses and treatments as any of the staff. With so much going for her, how could Jackie fail to get whatever she needed?

Just in the nick of time they had the machine and bed ready, as the doctor returned with a broad smile on his face and a giggling ten-year-old girl clinging to his back.

'All A-OK. Bang on target.' He was looking very pleased with himself and visibly relieved.

Easing Jackie on to the bed and getting ready to connect the tubing for the dialysis, Catherine felt the contagion of his high spirits. Could he have doubted his own skill? Surely not. She hadn't. 'Has Mrs Lasaria come with you?' she asked.

'Just outside. She doesn't want to see the connecting.' He eyed the machine dials carefully, noting the dialystate concentration. 'Right, that should do for starters. Now where did I put those X-ray films? I want to take another look.'

Catherine broke off her quiet explanations to Jackie about what she was doing. 'There's a viewing screen in the office.' She saw the little girl's mother watching from a distance and smiled. 'It looks as if the patient's relative carried your films for you.'

'Oh, right — I forgot. Many thanks.' He strode over to Mrs Lasaria just as Mrs Murphy was approaching with a determined air.

'Now don't you worry about all this, m'dear. Piece of cake, it is. See this round thing with the arrow? Well, it's a clock. When it goes off, she's done. Just like a cooker, it is.'

Catherine met Matt's eyes during this rapid and ingenuous description of state-of-the-art medical technology. It was impossible to resist the definite twinkle she saw there, and she suppressed a giggle, before turning back to her task.

Whatever the professionals might think of Mrs

Murphy's approach to a nervous mother, it worked perfectly, and Catherine allowed her to talk unchecked.

'Now it's this little thingy, hidden in the middle, that does the washing of all the nasty stuff in her blood, like — well, like one of those filter things in a washing machine. That's what it is, really. 'Cept it's the blood what gets washed, going in here and comin' out here.'

Both Jackie and her mother were listening with fascination as they saw the clear tubes fill with red fluid.

'There it goes, see? And it comes back all clean and fresh. Takes some of that puffy stuff away too. You won't be so fat-faced any more, will you, my pet?' smiled Mrs Murphy.

The little girl nodded. She had heard all the explanations before, but never quite like this. 'I hope not. The other kids call me. . .names.'

Mrs Murphy bridled with motherly indignation. 'Well, it shows how stupid they are, then. Now you just sit yourself down here, dear,' she settled Mrs Lasaria near the bed, 'and we'll keep watch and maybe read a bit, eh?' She found another chair for herself. 'We'll be all right, Nurse. My old hubby won't be here for ages yet, and we'll call you if we need anything.'

Feeling as if she had been effectively and summarily dismissed, Catherine smiled warmly at Mrs Murphy. The patient might have a proprietorial attitude to this machine, but she did know as much about how it worked as any technician and was capable of answering a mother's questions better than any scientist. She nodded at Jackie's mother, who was now beginning to look more relaxed. 'Everything should be fine, but if you want me to come, I won't be far away,' she told her.

'Thank you, Nurse. And thank the doctor, please? I forgot, I was so nervous.'

'I'll do that. And if you want tea or anything, Mrs Murphy can show you where everything is.' Catherine grinned at her self-appointed helper and left to start clearing up used surgical equipment.

Once everything was tidy she made a quick round of the unit, finding everything quiet. Emily had positioned herself with a mound of paperwork in Jackie's room and was chatting casually with another patient while keeping an eye on the little girl's first haemodialysis from a discreet distance. She nodded at Catherine's gesture and answered with an understood signal.

If Emily knew where she was, Catherine felt she could take a few minutes away to soothe the rumbling in her stomach with an early lunch. Jackie's treatment would be short, not much more than an hour, and a little time alone would be a pleasure. The tension of the morning was beginning to slip away in the wake of a growing sense of a new feeling. It might be hope, she thought. A hope that something might really happen. For Jackie, or——

'Time for a break?'

Catherine was passing the glass-fronted office and stopped. Matthew Dunnegan was sitting at the high counter, his pen poised over a set of clinical notes. She thought he would have left by now. 'Well, yes. . .'

'Good, wait for me. Won't be a sec.' With a flourish he scribbled a few more words and closed the buff folder before bouncing up to come round the opened door. 'Time for eats?'

His strong fingers had closed around her elbow and Catherine felt herself propelled down the corridor. He seemed filled with overflowing energy and happiness that spread through her arm, matching her own bubbles of light-heartedness.

'Not so fast!' she tried to remonstrate.

'I'm hungry,' was the unsympathetic reply. 'What's

in the kitchen, do you think? In my vast experience of ward kitchens there's always something hanging about, waiting to be eaten by starving doctors.'

The man is a food freak, she thought as she watched him examine the newly arrived lunch trays. 'You can't steal from the patients!' she protested.

'It's not stealing. Just checking everybody's diets, that's all.' Matt was lifting the plastic lid from every tray in turn. 'Ah, now Mr Petrussi really shouldn't have two desserts, even if he did order them. He mustn't overload his calcium, he's already hypercalcaemic.' A small rice pudding was liberated from the unsuspecting patient. 'Now, does Mr Browne really need that lasagne?'

'Yes, he does.' Catherine had to admit he had been right about Mr Petrussi's weakness for creamed puddings, but if he continued this way, no patient would have any lunch left. 'If you must indulge in petty pilfering, you can take the leftovers in the fridge.'

'Hm. But what if the cupboard is bare? Nothing here but a year's supply of antibiotics. Not too nutritious.' The dark head was deep inside the tall refrigerator. 'Well, maybe this, but I don't know.' He pulled out three plastic-covered sandwiches. 'They look a bit tired, but they'll have to do.' He added three eggs saved from unused breakfast trays and looked around. 'There must be a microwave somewhere.'

'Courtesy of Mrs Blessington.' Catherine pointed to the corner, hoping he wouldn't notice the adhesive strip on the side, giving the body temperature they used for warming the peritoneal dialysis bags. This was not exactly the approved method of heating the solutions.

His quick laugh dashed her futile hope. 'Hah! Not a bad way of heating; not all our methods are so different. Now, to create something vaguely edible. . .'

Surely he wasn't going to cook! Catherine retrieved her neatly packed lunch bag from the refrigerator as Matt cracked the eggs into a cereal bowl, wisked them rapidly and searched for their milk supply, muttering, 'No ward can function in this country without endless cups of milky tea,' added a splash, with a pinch of seasoning from the row of pepper shakers on the shelf.

At least no one here can have extra salt, Catherine thought as she found a high-backed chair and sat down to watch him create wonders out of nothing. There was no doubt in her mind that he would do precisely that; even the sunlight edging through the high window seemed to be dancing with invisible exhilaration.

Now he was looking for microwave dishes. She pointed. 'Over there.' It was a pleasure to see him move so easily and smoothly around her, as if he could take command wherever he was and make even their small kitchen come alive with activity. He was making her even hungrier, and she began to open her lunch.

'Great! Now we have a zap on high.' Turning the dials, Matt pushed a button before looking hopefully at Catherine. 'I don't suppose you've got anything going spare in that little goody-bag of yours?'

He was smiling longingly at the foil-wrapped square in her hands. She could hardly refuse to share, and that egg mixture had begun to look appetising. 'There's only cheese——'

'Perfecto!' A sharp *ping* made them both laugh. It was the same sound as Mrs Murphy's unintentional interruption. Matt liked the light of laughter in those hazel eyes, but returned his attention to the addition of Cheddar to his impromptu omelette. 'Another zap and we should be done. Where do we eat?'

'In the lecture-room, usually. We just use the empty tables.'

'Fine. Off you go and pick out the best one. I'll bring

the food along.' Matt waved her off as he started opening cupboards.

Making her way to the end of the corridor, Catherine glanced into the room where Mr Petrussi was sitting up, looking for his lunch tray. Poor man; he wasn't going to get everything he had ordered, but Matthew Dunnegan had been right about his calcium level. She wondered if the man with the deceptively easygoing manner ever missed anything or forgot even the smallest detail. He probably memorised those unending columns of figures on his blessed computer.

She laid out the remainder of her meal — two ripe tomatoes, an orange, a granary roll and a packet of raisins. Now that the cheese had disappeared, there didn't appear to be much left. She hoped he might share just a little bit of his eggs.

Matt arrived before she had laid out her depleted collection, his tray loaded with plates and cutlery. 'It's all in the presentation. And the company, of course.' He began to set down a steaming portion of browned omelette, with a separate plate of warm rolls and a sliced apple. 'Ah, tomatoes. How did you guess?'

Catherine merely nodded as he sliced the red globes into paper-thin wafers, placing half beside her eggs and half beside his.

'Fit for a king!' Tucking a paper towel under his chin, Matt viewed his handiwork. 'Not bad for leftovers, eh?'

'It looks good.' And smells even better, she thought as she followed his example and tried a mouthful. It was like filling her mouth with a savoury cloud that melted against her tongue. 'S'wonderful!'

'Shouldn't talk with your mouth full. First eat, then we talk.'

Matt was thinking as fast as he was eating. He had remembered her comment about eating on the unit, and rearranging his theatre list to fit in a catheter insertion had not been difficult, but now he had to use the rare opportunity of having this auburn-haired beauty in a place where she wasn't likely to let fly with a punch or a blunt object.

The main problem was the identity of the man who had given her those exotic earrings — someone who knew her better than she knew herself. He had ruled out the freckle-faced tennis partner, although that lad might come in useful. No, there was someone else. Someone who knew how gold reflected those tiny glints in hazel eyes. He'd try his doting father theory. 'How come you live in that mausoleum of a residence?' he asked.

'I like it,' Catherine answered rapidly before popping a large chunk of roll in her mouth.

'Where's home?'

She pointed to her mouth and shook her head.

Matt leaned back in his chair and waited until she had extracted every microscopic molecule of nutrition, and then, before she could take another bite, asked, 'So, where's home?'

'Here. Wherever I hang my hat, as they say.' She had managed to break off another piece of roll and punctuated her answer by filling her mouth. He obviously wanted to ask personal questions, and for some reason she didn't want him to delve too deeply.

Keeping his tone one of casual interest, Matt put a bowl of rice pudding decorated with raisins and orange segments before her as he asked, 'And your parents, where are they?'

'At the moment they're in Switzerland; last month they were in Italy.' That was easy enough to answer.

Those earrings had looked Mexican, or maybe further south. He asked, 'Have they been in South America?'

'No. Why?'

So much for the fond parent idea! Matt slowly finished his pudding. He was right back where he had started. 'Just wondering. It sounds like you have a well-travelled family.'

'It was their work; they were in the Diplomatic Service. Now they're doing just what they like.' Catherine watched the grey eyes looking thoughtfully out of the window. There was something endearing about that odd bump on his nose. It made him look like a little boy, trying to puzzle out something he couldn't yet understand. She wondered what he was thinking. She asked suddenly, 'Why did you come here?'

'I like new places and people that I've never seen before.' He turned back towards her. 'I get to do the work I care about. . .' he paused as if about to add something, then changed his mind and grinned '. . .and you never can tell just what you're going to find when you peek around that next corner. Whatever it is, it's bound to be different from what you expected.'

'How are we different?' queried Catherine.

Matt paused. There were some facts he was discovering that were not his to share, but there were more important differences, such as the feelings he was experiencing. These new sensations were centred on the delicately modelled face framed in a warm cloud of chestnut waves now lying softly against a sun-glowing cheek. It was better to veer away from close examination of such thoughts; he didn't want to lose that look of interest. 'Have you ever heard of the Gambro Mini Minor dialyser?' he asked.

At her shake of the head, he launched into a description of recent developments in paediatric haemodialysis, and was rewarded with rapt attention. At least he knew he was on safe ground here. He had seen the expertise and genuine caring in her work with Jackie; any information to do with patient care would be welcome.

In this guess he was only partly right. Catherine listened with a niggling sense of dismay. They had been so excited about their one new machine, but the techniques Matt Dunnegan was describing were on the opposite side of the world.

Hearing a soft sigh, Matt stopped and reached across to lightly touch her hand. 'Sorry, I' was waxing too lyrical! The patients stay the same, you know, even if the machinery keeps changing.'

'Yes, I know.' Catherine allowed her hand to remain under his, conscious of the indefinable comfort he was offering. 'You must have your share of Mrs Murphys and Jackies.'

'Ah, now, let me tell you about a young chap by the name of Bennie. Bennie Winterbottom. . .'

As he talked about a child with the improbable name, Catherine didn't know if he was inventing his story, but a tale of disappearing catheters, tantrums involving lost pyjama bottoms and emptied feather pillows associated with using a dialysis machine as aeroplane controls had her giggling. When he came to the use of a football in an impromptu bowling alley down a hospital ward, she held up her hand. 'Are all Americans as crazy as you?'

Matt appeared to consider this for a moment. 'Probably. I guess we're brought up not to accept anything as being unalterable.' His grin spread a mischievous glint across his face. 'We figure anything can be accomplished if we just try hard enough.'

His grin was infectious, and Catherine muttered, 'Miracle Matts all over the country.'

'That was just kid stuff.' He hoped she wasn't going to bring that up again.

Now he was looking positively sheepish, and Catherine pressed her advantage. 'So tell me then, what's a Wabash Cannonball? Another football play?'

She was surprised by the roar of laughter he let out as he leaned back, threatening to tip over in his chair. For a moment, she thought he was going to choke before he made a grab for the table ledge and pulled himself upright. 'You. . .really want to know?' he spluttered.

'I think so.' He was looking distinctly roguish, and she wondered what she had got herself in for.

She didn't have long to wonder, as Matt slowly stood, stretched to his full height, and took a deep breath before letting out the first notes of the rollicking song she had heard drifting down from the attic on Sunday afternoon. But now it was closer and much, much louder.

There was no stopping him, and Catherine listened, entranced. She knew he would have done exactly the same thing, no matter where he was or when. He was funny and brash and filled with life. Nothing would ever stop him from conquering anything or anyone he chose. The thought was exhilarating, and his exuberant serenade brought tears of laughter to her eyes as well as something else, undefinable but a quite lovely feeling.

The sound of clapping and laughter greeted the end of his song, and as Catherine felt him bow over her hand, she looked towards the door. Most of the ward staff had gathered to witness the loud performance, and Catherine blushed to see Emily's wide approving smile and Eileen Smythe's interested and amused gaze.

Matt's lips were brushing her hand, and Catherine pulled away quickly. 'Thank you. . .for the lunch.' She caught his eyes and added, 'It really was good, Matt.'

As she said his name, his face lit up like a beacon,

and Catherine lowered her glance to the littered table. 'I'll do the tidying, if you need to check Jackie.'

'You're the boss,' Matt whispered before he approached the admiring group at the door. There was no mistaking the bounce in his step or the lilt in his voice as he spread his arms wide. 'Ah, my admiring public! Now, fair Smitty, lead on to my duties in your domain of healing and redemption to deliver ease of suffering—and perhaps another look at those dialysate readings?'

The murmur of pleased rebuke from the unit sister could be heard under the nurses' voices as they all followed the surgeon back to the ward. The renal unit rarely had such entertainment, and Matt Dunnegan was well on his way to becoming part of the folklore of their small world.

No, he would not be forgotten easily, Catherine thought as she gathered up their empty plates. Other assistants had come and gone without so much as a ripple, but not this one. He caused gigantic waves wherever he went, and waves caused floods, and floods were destructive. He would have to be forgotten; he would leave when his contract finished, like the others. She did some quick addition. He was just completing the time of whatever-his-name-was who had stayed only three months. So Mr Dunnegan would be gone after Christmas. Better not to think of that. Better to remember the energy and vitality and the ridiculous songs.

She was humming the melody as she got home to her room in the residence that evening. Matt had disappeared back to his theatre list by the time she had returned to see Jackie off home. The effect of his presence had seemed to linger in the smiles and quickened steps of the staff as well as patients as the unit cleared for the weekend.

There was another postcard waiting for her, and she read Mark's message with a smile. 'Still digging up old relics. Anything new in your life I should know about? Hope earrings suit. May deliver Xmas prezzie in person, can't tell yet. Love, M.' He always knew more about her than she knew herself. She looked at the picture of a Mayan hieroglyphic calendar.

'Could you make sense of Matt Dunnegan?' she asked the distant man. 'Could you dig around in his head like those ruins of yours? What would you find, I wonder?'

There was no answer to such questions, and Catherine looked around her cosy nest with a critical eye. Some people seemed destined to explore new worlds, but others needed to stay put. There was a lot to be said for familiarity, she thought as she began to sort out laundry. Predictability could be very comfortable, if occasionally just a little bit dull.

CHAPTER SEVEN

'I THOUGHT he said he didn't play?'

The man sitting beside Danny answered, 'With that partner, I wouldn't mind a game or two of something.' A sharp dig in the ribs from his girlfriend silenced him, but Danny turned to Catherine.

'Who *is* that?' he demanded.

'You know him,' she answered with some asperity. They had been waiting for their first game in the tournament before all eyes had been drawn to the couple standing at the entrance to the court.

It wasn't only the glaring whiteness of their immaculate outfits that made Catherine narrow her eyes. Matthew Dunnegan was smiling and nodding at unfamiliar faces as he guided the petite brunette with the closely cropped black hair to a seat. The girl's short — very short — pleated skirt and short-capped blouse showed off her generous curves to advantage, and Catherine glanced down at her own tracksuit. It was a bright yellow, and together with Danny's navy blue shorts and red T-shirt, they made a colourful contrast to the newcomers.

'Not *him*, her!'

Catherine did not turn around to follow his admiring gaze. 'I don't know. Come on, Danny.'

As she headed confidently out to the court she was brought up short by the sight of Matthew Dunegan following her. What was he doing?

'There's been a change of game plan, Cath.' Danny was bouncing a tennis ball with exaggerated casualness against his ankle. 'Seems the rota's been changed. We've got a new team — ah. . .'

'This is Geraldine Duffy. Glad to see you again.' Matt was pumping Danny's hand as he grinned at Catherine. 'Hope we can give you a good match.'

'Sure. Glad to meet you.' Danny could hardly keep his eyes off the diminutive girl, and Catherine watched the tall man in his brand new pristine shorts, shirt and oversized trainers. Just what was he playing at? She had a good idea it wasn't tennis, but now he had trotted back to the service line and was attempting to hit slow volleys across the net.

'Shouldn't be a problem here,' she muttered to Danny as they started their warm-up. They had won the staff trophy twice in three years, and she doubted if this latest addition to the competition would change their prospects of victory.

'Better give it our best shot.'

True to his word, Danny astonished Catherine by playing as if they were in the All England finals, covering the court at speed, reaching for everything and displaying skills he usually reserved for their more demanding games.

All she had to do was stay at the net and send every volley out of the reach of the slow-footed man across from her. Catherine kept her eyes fastened on Matt as he bounded energetically after every shot even vaguely aimed in his direction. He was probably the worst tennis player she had ever seen in the club, but there was nothing wrong with his superbly muscled body.

It was hard to keep her eyes off the rippling thighs that flashed by her as he lunged at an impossible slice from Danny. His inevitable failure brought only a quick smile of flashing white teeth and a cheerful, 'Worth a try, eh?'

Catherine shook her head at him. 'Try staying

MILLS & BOON

Discover
FREE BOOKS
AND
FREE GIFTS
From Mills & Boon

As a special introduction to
Mills & Boon Romances we will send you:

16 FREE Mills & Boon Romances
plus a **FREE TEDDY** and **MYSTERY GIFT** when you
return this card.

But first - just for fun - see if you can find and circle four
hidden words in the puzzle.

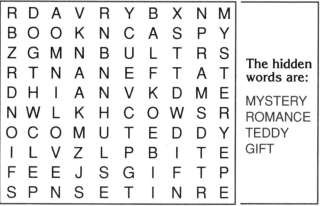

R	D	A	V	R	Y	B	X	N	M
B	O	O	K	N	C	A	S	P	Y
Z	G	M	N	B	U	L	T	R	S
R	T	N	A	N	E	F	T	A	T
D	H	I	A	N	V	K	D	M	E
N	W	L	K	H	C	O	W	S	R
O	C	O	M	U	T	E	D	D	Y
I	L	V	Z	L	P	B	I	T	E
F	E	E	J	S	G	I	F	T	P
S	P	N	S	E	T	I	N	R	E

**The hidden
words are:**

MYSTERY
ROMANCE
TEDDY
GIFT

Now turn over to claim your
FREE BOOKS AND GIFTS

Free Books Certificate

Yes Please send me FREE and without obligation 16 specially selected Mills & Boon Romances, together with my FREE teddy and mystery gift. Please also reserve a special Reader Service subscription for me. If I decide to subscribe, I shall receive 16 superb Romances every month for just £28.80, postage and packing FREE. If I decide not to subscribe I shall write to you within 10 days. The FREE books and gifts will be mine to keep in any case. I understand that I am under no obligation whatsoever. I may cancel or suspend my subscription at any time simply by writing to you. I am over the age of 18.

11A3R

FREE TEDDY

MYSTERY GIFT

Ms/Mrs/Miss/Mr

Address

Postcode

back. . .' She shut her lips together. What was she doing, helping the opposition? It was obvious that he had the power in those broad shoulders to hit the ball anywhere he chose if only he could get his feet moving, but he almost stumbled every time he ran forward. How could he be so uncoordinated? Josh's hero looked as if he had feet of clay, at least when he moved towards her. On the other hand, he was pretty good when he moved backwards. Was that what American footballers did?

As the games piled up in their favour, Catherine found she had little to occupy her thoughts, except pictures of Matt Dunnegan running backwards, and when he lifted his arm to power a serve she could see how he just might be able to throw something a long distance. Too bad he didn't know which end of a racquet was which.

Her partner was continuing to give a demonstration of flying determination, regardless of the lack of contest. It was only a matter of time before this upstart couple was sent packing to the dressing-rooms, and Catherine turned to suggest he save his energy. It was at that moment that an expert lob from the girl caught Danny unawares and he overreached himself, crashing to the floor with a strangled cry. 'Ow oh, heck jeez, I thought. . . Ow!'

Before she could reach his side a white form came hurtling over the net and was beside the fallen man, kneeling and gently prodding the leg bent under a groaning Danny.

'What happened?' asked Catherine, thinking that Matt Dunnegan might have been better to take up high jumping. He could move fast enough when he chose, and now he was nodding at Danny.

'Probably your ankle, lad. How's the shoulder?'

Long supple fingers were pressing against Danny's upper arm.

'OK, I think, but this hurts. . .'

'Oh, I'm so sorry. . . Danny.' A pair of wide brown eyes was looking down at them. 'I didn't mean——'

'No problem really.' Danny tried manfully to sit up. 'Ouch! I just tripped. Stupid, really.'

It was Matt who cut through this mutual self-incrimination. 'We'll need transport.' He thought for a moment before looking up at Catherine. 'How about Carlos's trolley? Think you could find it?'

She nodded and set off at a quick jog. Anything that could carry a heavy jukebox could carry Danny; there were no wheelchairs at the club; one question to the bar manager was enough to locate the cumbersome vehicle. By the time they had pushed it back towards the court they found Danny sitting in a plastic chair, his leg supported by an improvised splint formed from two tennis racquets bound with knotted ties.

'Pretty good, eh?' His face showed pain, but he tried to smile at Catherine. 'Sorry about this, Cath. Seems our trophy has gone.'

'Don't be silly, Danny. That's not important,' she answered. 'Now, how do we get you on to this thing? Oh, no——'

Before she could finish her thought, Matt had lifted Danny, his chair and his splints on to the trolley and was balancing the weight against his chest. 'Carlos, do you think——'

'Sure, Dr Matt. Shove over, *amigo*.'

And so they set off out of the club through lines of curious onlookers—a procession centred on a giant goods trolley bearing a smiling Danny who began to offer royal waves with the one hand that was not being held by a worried-looking Geraldine.

'It'll have to be the service entrance. No stairs.' Matt

was not even breathing heavily as he indicated to Carlos to steer to their left near the main hospital. As the pub manager's puffing became more audible, the trolley proceeded smoothly through the basement, weaving a path through piles of discarded hospital equipment.

'It's so creepy down here!' Geraldine kept a firm hold on Danny's hand.

'*Si*, is dark.' Carlos looked around cautiously. 'Is where they keep the bodies, *no*?'

Catherine smiled. 'No, Carlos. The mortuary is way over on the other side.'

'Oh!' A quiet squeak from Geraldine brought a soft whisper from Matt.

'Go easy on the civilians, my lovely. Not everyone loves the mysteries of these temples of healing as we do.' He raised his voice. 'Now turn right, Carlos. Elevators are around the corner.'

His cheerful smile and a, 'Sorry, ma'am,' brought a medical records clerk with her overloaded metal push-cart to a standstill in front of the opening lift doors and she stood aside to watch them all pile into the confined space.

Catherine said, 'Thanks,' to the clerk and smiled. Now the story of this escapade would be all over the hospital within hours and the Matt Dunnegan legend would be embellished with each telling, but she had to admit that however unorthodox their means of trans-port, he had brought Danny to where he needed to be—Casualty.

'Sorry, Carlos—I forgot.' Matt turned to his sturdy assistant pusher. 'We'll need our gear from the club——'

'I'll get it, Dr Matt.' Carlos was already pulling at his empty trolley as Danny settled himself into a wheelchair. 'Worth a couple of free drinks when you get back, all this, eh?'

A laugh and a wave of his hand was the only response as Matt disappeared behind the swing doors. Geraldine was looking around at the few people waiting patiently to be seen.

'Do you want to come in with us, or wait here?' asked Catherine.

'Oh, I'll wait, please.'

Hearing the reluctance in the girl's voice, Catherine remembered what Matt had said. It was true that not everyone who worked in a hospital was comfortable in a busy clinical area. 'Fine. I'll see if I can rustle up a cup of tea.' She smiled as she added casually, 'Do you work in one of the offices here?'

Geraldine answered the smile. 'Yes. I'm good with paperwork, but it's hard to get used to all this.' She waved a hand around at the waiting-room. 'I'm the PA to the transplant co-ordinator on the third floor.'

'Really?' Danny had manoeuvred his chair next to her. 'That's great! I work in the labs, and we——'

A new voice briskly interrupted them. 'Right then, what do we have here? Broken bones? At least you've picked the quiet time before the pub punch-ups start coming in.'

Catherine nodded at the casualty officer, whose face she recognised; he had apparently been summoned from the depths of the accident and emergency department, and she wondered where Matt had got to now. So his pretty girlfriend just happened to work in the transplant office, where she could supply the codes to add to a certain doctor's little red book. For some reason, this thought gave her a tiny twinge of relief that was quickly suppressed.

As she pushed Danny into a curtained cubicle Catherine took a quick look around. All the staff were busy tending unseen occupants in other cubicles, but there was no one in the two side rooms and the accident area was empty. She might as well stay to help, at least until her presence became a hindrance.

Danny grunted as he slid up to the hard examination bed. 'Hope I don't need any of that.' His eyes indicated the walled outlets of gases, sphygmomanometer and luridly coloured push-buttons.

'I doubt it, mate. My name's Frank. Did I hear you say you worked in the labs?' The young house officer was repeating Matt's examination of Danny's ankle.

While Danny was being distracted by the casual conversation, Catherine removed his socks and shoes, positioned him as comfortably as possible with the adjustable headrest before remembering her promise to Geraldine. 'Time to hunt for the teapot. Is that OK, Frank?'

'Sure — add another bag for me. Now, how about the shoulder. . .or wrist? Ah, now this looks promising.'

The casualty officer might be young, but he knew how to deal with anxious patients with unexpected injuries, and Catherine knew Danny was in good hands. Finding the staff-room was no problem. She followed the smell of fresh coffee and found the makeshift kitchen with signs of recent habitation. After preparing a large pot of tea, knowing that anyone who entered would help themselves, she went to sit with Geraldine.

Trying a few indirect comments, Catherine discovered that the girl was less interested in talking about Matt Dunnegan than Danny and the severity of his injuries. The doctor had been kind and interested in her work — Catherine could well believe that — but he was overshadowed in importance by the crumpled form of Danny. 'Now you two won't be able to play in the tournament, and he's such a good player.'

A caustic and unflattering comment about the comparison of Matt Dunnegan with any other tennis player hovered on Catherine's lips but remained unspoken as the casualty officer arrived to invite Geraldine to sit with Danny.

'You look as scared as he does, so why don't you commiserate with each other? Go on, it's OK. He'll be off to X-Ray soon, and you can go along as well.'

'Thank you.' Geraldine gave them both a grateful smile.

'Straight ahead.' Frank pointed the girl in the right direction and turned to Catherine. 'He seemed worried about his girlfriend. Now, where's that tea you were talking about?'

Leading the way to the kitchen, Catherine poured a generous mugful and handed it to him.

'Great stuff! Keeps the neurons from shrivelling to bits.' He dragged out a battered cake tin. 'Should have some old biscuits somewhere. Need a sugar jar as well.' He started to munch. 'A few minutes' respite. I hope Matt finds himself a radiologist—they're a scarce breed on weekends around here.'

Catherine asked, 'Is that where Mr Dunnegan went?'

'Mr. . .? Oh, yeah. Down here he's just Matt. Almost one of the regulars, and thank God for that.'

'Oh?' she queried.

The young doctor eyed Catherine closely. 'I've seen you around. Dressed a bit differently, though.' He grinned at her embarrassed tug at her canary-coloured tracksuit. 'Where is it you work?'

'Over in the dialysis unit.'

'Then you'll understand.' Frank settled himself more comfortably, dragging over a low coffee table to balance his feet, which Catherine was amused to see encased in scuffed trainers. 'He first came to check our supply of donor cards, found us sadly lacking in our duties regarding organ donation and took it on. Better him than me.'

Catherine sipped at her tea. Yet again, Matt Dunnegan had found an area of hospital territory where he had made himself at home. 'What do you mean?' she asked.

'He talks to relatives of RTAs, sudden deaths, that sort of thing. Close to the motorway here we have a fair supply of candidates, unfortunately.' Frank shrugged. 'He doesn't give up easily, I'll say that for him. I wouldn't have the guts.'

'What do you mean?' she queried.

'He'll spend hours with these folks—you know, the bereaved, the families in shreds with their boy on life support with no vital signs, hopeless. Motorcycles mostly. Nothing we can do. Not a dicky bird.' He glanced at Catherine's face. 'Yeah, it sounds gruesome and it is. But you know how much your people need donors, and he's here on the front line, doing his damnedest to get them.'

Not knowing what to say, Catherine kept silent. She did know the difficulty of obtaining cadaver transplants, but preferred not to think about it. Matt Dunnegan couldn't do that.

Frank had his hands curled around the warm tea mug. 'He's really good. Sometimes he doesn't get consent, but the relatives always seem to feel better after he talks to them. Some time I'd like to sit in and see how he does it, but the time. . .well, our job seems to be different.' He sighed. 'Especially with the kids, he's best then. Must be god-awful.'

'Kids?' Was he searching for a paediatric donor? It had to be for Jackie.

'Yeah. He spent four hours with a young couple last Monday night. Four hours, would you believe? Their boy was only eight, a bicycle hit by a lorry and no helmet.'

She had to ask. 'Did they consent?'

Frank took a sip before answering. 'I don't know. The boy went up to Intensive Care on ventilation with all the tubes. We got busy and I never followed it up. But the parents, I remember them. Looked as if they'd had a ray of hope after Matt left. Whatever he said to them, it helped.' He began to straighten up. 'Makes our lives a lot easier, does Matt. I'm glad he's here.'

As the unmistakable sound of an ambulance siren keened in the distance they both looked at each other, and Frank nodded at Catherine. 'The sound of our approaching mortality. That's another thing about Matt. He's not bashful about lending a hand with cardiac resuscitation when needed. Both sides of the coin, so to speak.' He stretched his arms above his head. 'You make a good cuppa, but it sounds as if I'm about to be called back to the fray. Can you check on your friend for me? He'll probably be OK with a walking plaster, but there might be a Colles' fracture as well. Matt can read the films if a radiologist doesn't materialise.'

They both rinsed out their cups and Catherine made her way to Danny's cubicle. She could see personnel gathering at the Accident entrance, already checking equipment as a nurse talking on the telephone passed on information being given by the ambulance driver in staccato bursts of quiet instructions.

Geraldine was standing outside the cubicle nervously shifting her feet.

'Is anything wrong?' asked Catherine.

'I don't think so,' the petite girl answered. 'Matt said he wanted to talk to Danny alone for a few minutes. I hope it doesn't mean anything?' she ended on a note of query, as if Catherine could offer reassurance.

Seeing a hospital porter walking steadily towards them through the busy staff in the accident-room, Catherine guessed there was no difficulty in getting the X-rays; she couldn't think what Matt and Danny needed to talk about in private.

'Got somebody here for X-ray?' The porter eyed them with an experienced look. Anyone out of uniform had to be a relative.

'In here.' Matt's voice came from behind the curtain, and as he emerged he revealed Danny already seated in a wheelchair. 'Dr Stephens should be waiting in the reporting-room. Left wrist, left tibia, ankle and foot. Here's the request form.'

'Right you are, Doc.' The porter was already swinging Danny back towards the public waiting-room and reached for the form to stuff in his shirt pocket. Even in that smart tennis gear, he knew a doctor when he saw one; he'd even seen one in his pyjamas once. You saw a bit of everything in A and E if you stuck around long enough. 'Let's be off, then, lad. See what bones you've managed to bust up.'

'Just a minute.' Danny put a restraining hand on one of the large wheels. 'You've got a deal, Matt. We can start on Monday, right?'

'First you have to get yourself up and around.' Matt added, with a quick glance at the two girls, 'We can talk later.'

Geraldine asked, 'Can I go along? You said——'

'Sure,' Matt smiled, and looked at Catherine steadily. 'Do you want to go with them?'

'No.' She had seen enough X-rays done, and there was something she wanted to ask. About an eight-year-old boy who had been in an accident.

The porter had had enough of chit-chat and moved Danny smartly down the hall, accepting the accompanying friend as an inevitable encumbrance to be ignored. He hoped she was a fast walker.

'At least he's not wasting time.' Matt was looking around. 'Did Carlos get our gear? I'd better get changed.'

Wondering what 'deal' Matt had struck with Danny, Catherine said, 'I'll take a look. There's tea in the staff-room if you want it.'

'Great, thanks.' With a quick nod, he made straight for the kitchen.

As she lugged the heavy canvas bags back into the staff-room from Reception where they had been left, Catherine knew the casualty officer had been speaking the truth. Matt Dunnegan moved around this department as if he owned it, and he was obviously getting ready to assist with whatever emergency was causing the loudly approaching siren.

She plunked his bag down and made herself another cup of tea. It would serve as an excuse to stay. And ask questions. 'Frank said you work down here a lot,' she said.

Matt was already unzipping his case. 'Hm, young Frank doesn't usually give out information so readily. You must have had your usual dazzling effect on him.'

She wasn't to be so easily distracted. 'He mentioned a little boy, but he didn't say what had happened to him.'

'Which one? We've had quite a few in lately. One covered in dog bites, another with thirty per cent burns from an overturned heater. . .' His voice became muffled as he drew his white cotton T-shirt over his head, and Catherine took a deep breath.

'This one was eight years old.' That bare expanse of chest was having an unnerving effect on her pulse rate. There was no doubt about the attractiveness of this particular male's physique. She tucked her legs securely underneath her on the wide chair; if she left now she would never learn what she wanted to know. About the boy. 'He had a bicycle accident.'

Matt started to splash water over his face and neck from the kitchen sink, his words separated by spurts of water blown through his hands. 'I remember. These things are murderous.' He was trying to dry himself with paper towels.

Catherine reached down to scrabble in her own case and threw him a towel. The sooner he dried himself the sooner that sinewed chest would disappear under another shirt.

'Ah, lovely and soft!' His eyes appeared over the edge of the fluffy fabric and gleamed at her. 'Just like you — all cuddly in that bunny outfit.'

Bunny? More like a giant butterball, she thought.

'I like butterballs.'

With a start, she realised she must have spoken out loud. 'You would. Anything to do with food!' Now he was beginning to unzip his shorts. She scrunched herself more deeply into the armchair. He wasn't making this any easier.

'Do you intend to watch quite so intently?' Matt paused in his actions.

Catherine knew her cheeks were flushed, but she answered calmly, 'Nothing I haven't seen before.'

He gave a quiet chuckle. 'Not precisely true, my lovely, unless I've missed something I surely would have remembered.'

The shorts were dropped to the floor, and Catherine lowered her gaze to the mug clenched in her fists, but not before she had a clear view of the slim hips tapering into the strongly muscled thighs she had imagined. Now that image was imprinted on her inner eye, and she gulped silently. Her abdominal muscles were starting a slow seductive dance around her ribcage and deep breathing wasn't helping. Beneath her fringed lashes she could see him reach for dark-coloured trousers, and she kept her eyes fastened on the bare feet being eased out of the boat-sized trainers. Only when brown socks and casual loafers had been safely slipped on did she venture to raise her eyes.

Now he was fully dressed, Catherine returned to the reason for her presence during this male stripper performance. 'What happened to him?' she asked.

Matt was neatly packing his discarded clothing into his sports bag. 'He didn't make it.'

'And. . .?'

'And what?' He adjusted his open-necked shirt. 'I should have a white coat, otherwise they'll think I'm a walk-in plumber.'

Her rising inner turmoil and what seemed his deliberate evasiveness was proving too much for Catherine. It was impossible to concentrate, and for some reason she was becoming extremely irritated. 'Did you *get* it?' she demanded.

Matt sat down on the coffee table facing her and gently took the empty mug from her tensed fingers. 'Simmer down, my sweet! I assume we're talking about donations here.'

There were tiny drops of water still clinging to the edge of his temples, and she felt an urge to touch a fingertip to the glistening skin so tantalisingly near. 'Yes, tell me — please!'

'All right, Catherine.' His voice remained quiet as his thumb made smooth circles around her inner palm. 'He never regained consciousness, but his parents had time with him, and that's what matters.'

The rhythmic movements against her skin were not as soothing as he might intend. 'And their consent? Did they give it?'

He nodded without taking his eyes from her face.

'Yes, they agreed. I think it gave them some comfort, in a strange sort of way.'

Catherine curled her fingers inside his grasp. 'Jackie? A match for her?'

'No way of knowing,' said Matt. 'There were too many crush injuries for major organ donation. They agreed to corneal removal, and the ophthalmology team did the harvesting.'

'Harvesting?' Catherine choked on the ugly word. It was horrible to think of human beings as nothing more than crops to be chopped down. She felt her eyes beginning to sting.

He lifted one hand to stroke the tangled curls beside the glistening long lashes. 'Now one, maybe two people can see the world again. That's not a bad thing.'

'No, it's not, but. . .' she wanted to bury her head in that strong steady shoulder '. . .nothing for Jackie.'

'No, not for Jackie.' He drew her closer and brushed his lips against her closed eyelids. 'Not yet. Don't give up hope, lovely Catherine. I haven't.'

'You never give up hope, do you? Old Miracle Matt.' The words were stifled in the folds of his freshly starched collar. It all seemed so hopeless. How could she wish another child to die so that Jackie should live? She reached up to bring his head closer; she needed to shelter against the bulwark that never cracked or weakened.

Matt curved his fingers under her chin and lifted her face from the hollow of his shoulder. 'There are different kinds of miracles.' He moulded his lips against hers, deepening his pressure until the well of welcome opened and he tasted the thrill of her desire matching each of his tiny searching thrusts.

Catherine clung to the source of energy filling her inner being with liquid fire, allowing herself to float on the waves of pleasure each delicious movement brought, curling against his all-encompassing strength.

'Catherine, my lovely. . .'

Words murmured against her neck seemed to come from a great distance, and Catherine felt his hands reaching to hold her closer. She let out a tiny mew of delight as his fingers brushed her breast instantly surging under his touch. 'Matt. . .'

The feel of her warm skin under his hands was like molten honey, and Matt held her pressed against a heart drumming so hard that he was deafened. 'You're the miracle, you know that. . .' He remembered that half-lidded look at his body, the brief glance that had given him the courage to reach out for the wonder of her. 'Perfection of beauty is always to be worshipped. . .' He wanted to touch, kiss, caress every part of her. 'Wondrous, glorious woman!' He buried his face in the sweetly scented hair falling back from her arched neck. 'My lovely, lovely butterball!'

She wanted to laugh with pure happiness, but all she managed was a strangled giggle as she tried to lock her arms around his neck. 'Speaking of glorious. . .' She had been about to make a remark about his physical attributes, but she felt a tension in his body. 'What's the matter?'

'Don't know.' Matt pressed a feathery kiss on her forehead as he turned to listen.

Catherine slackened her hold, but continued to lean against the shoulder enfolding her in warm solidity. She frowned; something was different, but she couldn't tell what. . . Yes, she knew. There was no sound. There was only silence.

CHAPTER EIGHT

'It's stopped.'

'The siren? Yes. But not this.' Matt's mouth moved slowly across her face. 'This. . .' he touched her nose '. . .is. . .' a delicate tracery crossed her chin '. . .to be continued.' He nibbled gently at her lower lip.

The sudden stillness had brought Catherine back to reality; the raucous scream of the siren had been an echo of her own sensations, and now it had ended. She trailed a finger across the odd bump on his nose. It was such a lovely nose. She murmured, 'Who did this?'

Matt laughed and lifted her fingertips to his lips. 'You mean before you? An over-energetic flying tackle. I didn't run fast enough.'

'I think you move quite fast enough.' Catherine smiled into the eyes glowing softly like half-buried charcoal embers. She reached down to readjust her disarrayed clothing, but found his hands in her way. 'We have to go — at least, you do.' To her chagrin she heard the unsteadiness in her own voice.

'Come with me?'

The intensity of his words gave them an added meaning, but Catherine merely attempted to slide off his lap. For an instant Matt held her tightly around the waist, then sighed softly and released her.

Catherine made an attempt to tidy her tumbled mass of hair. 'I'm hardly dressed to assist with cardiac massage!' She smiled to take any sting of rejection out of her words; she wasn't sure what he had been asking.

'You look fine to me. But that wasn't precisely——'

Whatever he had been about to say was lost as the

111

sound of metal banged against the outside wall and the casualty officer poked his head around the door. 'I could use your help, Matt. Maybe a couple of candidates for you, can't tell yet.'

'Bad?'

Catherine heard the resignation in Matt's response, whether for the extent of the emergency or something else, she couldn't tell.

'Yeah — multiple pile-up. Three critical, one DOA.' Frank waved a white lab coat through the doorway. 'All hands to the pump, as they say.'

Matt spoke crisply. 'Be right there.' As he shrugged into the uniform the public expected, he turned to Catherine. 'See you?'

She nodded, without speaking. She couldn't say what she was thinking — that at this moment the dead were more important than the living. Some poor person had arrived 'dead on arrival', and that meant that Matt was needed to ask the questions that his patients couldn't ask for themselves.

He raised his hand briefly as if to touch her cheek, but he dropped it and fumbled in the strange pocket as if looking for something that wasn't there.

'Good luck, Matt.'

Her words brought a flicker of a smile and an easing of the deep lines along his forehead. 'I hope I haven't used up my share. You're all the luck I want, Catherine.'

Before she could respond, he disappeared in the wake of the receding instrument trolley clanking towards the accident-room. She stood immobile for a moment before gathering up her sports bag and making an unseen exit through the waiting-room.

She needed time to think. It was easier to marshall her thoughts into some sort of order after closing her own door and flopping down on the bed. Hugging herself as if to hold on to the precious memory of warm hands and lips, she smiled softly. Whoever had invented tracksuits must have had the thought of athletic men in mind, especially a man who excited such miraculous feelings. Miracle Matt indeed! One kiss, in the A and E staff-room of all places, and she was acting like a lovelorn adolescent!

She sat up suddenly. Just the memory of Matt Dunnegan was giving her tingly feelings all over; it was impossible to stay still.. She wanted to dance and fling her arms around the whole world and sing. . . No, not sing. Matt did that for both of them, him and his cannonball. She let out a loud, long whoop trying to imitate a train whistle, but succeeded in sounding more like a drunken owl. She giggled and made a face at herself in the mirror.

Well, he's cannoned into you, that's for sure. Flattened you like a sixpence. The sparkling eyes looked back at her and she frowned, trying to dull the glee in that reflected image. Second thoughts were called for. One delicious snuggle did not indicate a declaration of undying love and devotion, especially with a man who moved with the speed of light. She needed to calm down, do something constructive instead of dreaming. Her eyes fell on the colourful Mexican picture. That was it! There was someone she could always talk to. She hunted for writing paper.

> Dear Mark, Today was our first game, but for me the competition is over. . .

The slight man was standing beside the reception desk, and Catherine brushed by him before recognition and surprise brought her back.

'Why, Josh, what are you doing here? Emily's not here. . .'

'I know.' He looked ill at ease and spoke in a rush. 'I just delivered more software, and Matt said I could. . . I mean, Em had to stay home with Seth 'cause of his cold, but she said you. . . Sorry.' He stopped at the look of confusion on her face. 'You busy?'

'Well, yes,' Catherine answered. Busy was an understatement. For some reason, all the patients had chosen this week to develop urinary infections or blocked fistulas, or in Mr Petrussi's case some new form of skin rash to keep them run off their feet. Being short-staffed didn't help, but she had been grateful for the workload. It had kept her mind off the lack of message from Matt Dunnegan. For six days it had been as if they had never even met, let alone. . .'What is it, Josh?' she asked.

'Do you have a little girl here named Jackie? Matt said — well, can I see her?'

'She's in the last room on the left.' Catherine didn't have time to ask questions. It was logical that Josh should be interested in the work if he was developing computer programmes, even if she didn't quite see what one patient would have to do with this. 'I'll have to leave you, Josh. I'm hunting for an acetate dialyser and I can't remember where I put it.'

As she darted off, Catherine thought he must think she was barmy; he wouldn't know what she was talking about. Matt Dunnegan would know, though. And he'd probably find it too, she thought as she made another search of the equipment-room. Her brain seemed to have become unusually fuzzy this past week.

Discovering that she had already positioned the dialyser in Mrs Murphy's machine, Catherine went to find Josh. He was standing outside the glass window looking down at the sleeping child. He turned at her approach.

'She's really pretty, isn't she?' he remarked.

Catherine agreed. 'She's much better now too. Matt's treatment change has really helped.'

'He said I could watch an operation. Do you think that would be all right?' asked Josh.

'If he says so.' Catherine wondered if Emily knew about her husband's new interest in medicine.

As if sensing her puzzlement, Josh explained, 'I've got a promotion—up to medical marketing. Now they've given me a car and put me on the team selling and developing Health Service programs, but there's so much I don't know yet. Is Matt operating today?'

'Only in the morning.' Catherine knew his exact theatre schedule by heart. 'It's Prof's list this afternoon.' She had a good idea. 'Do you want me to take you over? We need a special requisition filled from Central Supply, and it's in the same place as the theatres.' There might be a better way of spending her half-day off, but she couldn't think of any right now. It was likely that Matt would be assisting the professor, and she would at least see him if only from a distance.

Josh seemed relieved to have a guide to the hidden corridors of the surgical suite, and Catherine found him a seat in the empty observation gallery.

'It's so small,' he whispered.

'The operating-rooms on TV always look bigger,' she explained. 'And you don't need to whisper—they can't hear us.' She was glad to see that the patient was already on the table, anaesthetised and fully draped. There was no predicting Josh's reaction to the sight of the large incision needed for this surgery, and she settled beside him. More explanations might be needed. She had delivered her requisition slip and now she was on her own time, after all.

Her heart skipped a beat as a familiar form came into the brightly lit space. Even fully gowned and masked there was no mistaking the tall man who glanced up at the gallery, nodding briskly at Josh, then stared at Catherine for a second before lowering his eyes to the operating field.

Catherine felt a tiny chill at the look; it was as if he didn't want her here. If he had given Josh permission to watch, why should he object to her presence? Now he had positioned himself so his back was to the observers, his broad shoulders obstructing most of their view.

'Here comes the Prof.' Catherine pointed to the short figure walking slowly with his gloved hands clasped in front of him. 'Now they're making the first incision through the top muscle layers. The nurse is clamping off the first blood vessels.' She glanced at Josh to see his reaction to the inevitable blood loss, but he seemed fascinated. Pehaps Matt had been wise to limit their view of the proceedings.

She continued, 'It won't take them very long to reach the kidney, but it will be removed slowly after each connection is freed. Those are the retractors he's using to keep the area open. . .' Her commentary slowed and stopped. She couldn't be sure, but what she was seeing was not what she had expected to see. She leaned forward, trying to focus against the glare of the circular fluorescent lighting just above the surgeons' heads.

'Is that the kidney?' Josh asked with no hint of squeamishness. 'It's not very big, is it?'

Catherine took her eyes away from the gloved hands busy with clamps and swabs. 'No, no bigger than your fist, but if you look. . .' she indicated the container being prepared for histology '. . .there's a lump on it, probably a tumour. That might be why it's being removed.'

The movements of the surgical team had speeded up

as closure began, and as Catherine watched the professor leave there was a knock at the gallery door.

'Note for you, Miss Woodley.'

The scrap of paper was in Matt's tidy script, asking her to bring Josh to his office. There was nothing else, no please or thank you.

Even if he had not invited her, she would have gone. There were a few answers she needed to have; she hadn't liked what she had seen.

Josh was still watching the activity below them. 'That's a neat job, eh? Where does he go now?' he queried.

Assuming he meant the patient, Catherine said, 'He'll be in the recovery-room until he wakes up, then to Intensive Care for a while.' She showed the note to Josh. 'We've been summoned.'

'Good. I left some new stuff on his desk; maybe he's got some questions.'

He's not the only one, Catherine thought as she led the way to the floor above. The office was empty, and she sat down to wait while Josh tinkered with a new monitor he had apparently installed. Looking around, she could see several bits of new equipment. That drug research grant must have been generous.

'Sorry to keep you—last-minute details.' Matt came through the door at a fast jog and grinned at them both. His smile deepened as he looked at Catherine. 'Hello, my lovely. Can we have a word, Josh? Should be some coffee across the way, and I'm parched!'

The sight of that muscular form in flimsy cotton theatre shirt and trousers had brought back a sweet memory of tender loving, and Catherine tightened her uniform belt. She had purposely not changed before coming over; this was to be an entirely professional meeting, since Matt had not seen fit to make so much as a single telephone call. He wasn't the only one who could play a cool game.

There was no knowing how long he would be with Josh, and she looked idly over the pile of papers near her elbow. A thick fold of computer print-out sheets was topped with an array of lab results, and she recognised Danny's signature on several green forms. So that was what they had agreed; Danny was involved in Matt Dunnegan's research. She read the patient's name on the top form: Mr N. Saint.

Poor man! Catherine smiled to herself. Having a name like that must be a trial. She edged closer to the screen Josh had set up and looked at the unfamiliar menu. It was a program she had never seen before — but then that was what he was buying from Josh and probably discussing out of earshot. She looked at all the acronyms. There was the DIALAB file she had given him; the one underneath read TXNAME which was probably Geraldine's contribution, but she didn't recognise any of the others. At the very bottom was an odd code: SANTAS.

Guessing what it might be, she punched the code and found she was in a detailed record of Jackie's medical file. It was organised in a different way from the clinical notes but covered her entire medical history and all treatment since she had come to St Damien's. As she skimmed rapidly through the pages, Catherine realised how much work had gone into gathering all this data from so many different sources. Everything was here — all the results — hundreds of them — and reading the options at the bottom of the screen, Catherine saw they could all be mixed and matched, compared and correlated with each other in dozens of different ways. Josh had been ingenious.

The final page of the file was incomplete, with only cryptic notes for future action much as would be written in a normal medical note. One name caught her eye. It was Mr N. Saint again. There was a question mark beside the name, and Catherine reached for the green result form, with a growing sense of excitement.

The results were T and B cells, and she knew they were part of tissue-typing. Quickly she scrolled back to Jackie's results, done when she had first arrived. They were the same. Catherine held the form beside the screen to double check, and it was true. This Mr Saint had to be a donor!

She tried to ease the trembling in her hand and sat back. Matt had done it! He'd found a donor. Maybe it had been one of the accident victims last weekend; it would have taken this long to get the results. What if he didn't have consent? She looked at the form; it didn't say the man was deceased—but then he might not be. He might still be on life support.

The name Saint must be another code to preserve the anonymity of the donor. Of course! St Nicholas for Jackie. She began to smile. Only Matt would think of that; he had remembered the first thing the little girl had said to him, and now he had found the perfect gift for her, just what she had wished for.

She whirled around as the door opened behind her. As she tried to wave the green form and ask the important question, she was enfolded in a waft of hexachlorophene as strong arms crept around her shoulders.

'Mmm, you smell lovely.' Matt was nibbling gently under her ear, and Catherine squirmed against the tiny electric jolts his touch sent down her spine.

'Well, *you* don't!' She wriggled her nose against the strong odour of disinfectant emanating from his scrubbed skin, and keeping her eyes away from the sight of curly dark hair peeping above the deep V of his cotton top, tapped his nose with the request form. 'Is this it? Is this Jackie's donor?'

Matt frowned briefly and sighed. 'I forgot I'd left it there.' He took the form away from her and moved to lock it away in a drawer. 'Can we keep this to ourselves for a while, please?'

'But why? It's a match, isn't it? I checked——'

'You would!' He grinned wryly at her. 'For one thing, I don't have consent yet, and for another, all donors are supposed to be put into the pool.' He tapped the thick computer print-out pile. 'I'd like to keep this one for Jackie, if it's available.'

'Oh.' Catherine eyed the wad of names under his elbow. Another one of those thousands of waiting patients might be an even better match than Jackie; somehow the competition seemed all wrong.

'You see, I like to keep what I find.' Matt reached across to hold her hands. 'Especially when it's special.'

Resisting the urge to comment that a single phone call might do wonders if he was talking about her, Catherine kept her hands still. Not a single word had she heard from him, and here he was, looking as if he thought everything was perfect and they could pick up right where they had left off. There was a deep gleam in those grey eyes that was beginning to cause a familiar flutter under her ribcage. 'That depends on what you do, I suppose. Or don't do,' she added.

Matt looked puzzled, but continued to smile confidently. 'You're looking at your new partner, my lovely. Together we'll crush all opposition.'

'Partner?' she echoed. 'What are you talking about?'

'That trophy of yours. We're going to win it. Danny has the utmost confidence in me.' He was beaming at her.

Catherine was astonished. 'Tennis? You can't play tennis! You've got two left feet!'

He made a face at her surprise. 'Oh, ye of little faith! Even Geraldine sees some hope for me.'

'Then you can play with her!'

'Nope, don't want to. Besides, she's off on a management training course for a month.' Matt was keeping a firm hold on her hands.

Feeling the heat of irritation joining the tingling warmth spreading up her arms, Catherine hoped the absent Geraldine might be learning about how to keep the confidentiality of computer codes in the face of charming and handsome men exerting the full force of their persuasive powers. Such as now. She muttered, 'I don't care about the stupid trophy.'

'Well, I do. It should be yours, and Danny wants me to take over from him. You think I can't?' He lifted her palms to his lips.

Her defences were weakening, and she growled, 'You can probably take over from anyone you choose——' She stopped suddenly and pulled her hands away with a force that rocked him slightly. 'That's what you did today, isn't it?'

Matt lowered his gaze and sat back in his chair. He had tried to block her view, but he should have known better.

'That's what you did! You took over. That was supposed to be Prof's case, and you didn't let him get a look in, did you?' Catherine's anger grew as she remembered why she had come here.

'Well, I——'

'I'm not blind. I've seen a few nephrectomies before, you know.' The release of pent-up adrenalin felt good. 'Since when do honorary consultants take over from the department head, tell me that? Prof was left holding the retractors, and even that——' She stopped, trying to remember what she had seen.

Matt glanced at her but said nothing.

Catherine spoke more slowly. 'Even that was taken over, by the theatre sister.' She stared at the face turned away from her. 'Just what was going on? No one down there seemed to think anything was strange—just me. The Prof was there, it was his theatre list, but he didn't do anything. Why not?'

Matt shook his head slowly as he absentmindedly ruffled the edges of the computer sheets. He had no right to tell her, and he remembered his own feelings when he'd discovered what she was trying to explain. Her feelings were unlikely to be the same. 'It's my job to do whatever the Prof wants.' He added carefully, 'Or needs.'

'Needs?' A faint glimmer of a memory tugged at the edges of Catherine's mind, but she couldn't grasp it. She tried to reconstruct the activities beside the operating table. Nothing had been said. The sister had moved in without instruction to hold those large retractors. The professor's hands had been shaking, not enough for anyone unaccustomed to the positioning of the instruments to notice, but a slight trembling. 'He was a little shaky.'

As she said the words, the elusive detail fell into place. 'Oh, no, Matt, don't say it was for him! That drug—the prescription they sent to the unit by mistake, the Levodopa?'

Matt nodded slowly.

Icy fingers were closing around her lungs, and Catherine took a deep breath. 'He has Parkinson's?'

'I'm afraid so.' He confirmed her guess and kept talking to allow her time to think. 'He needed an increased dose and had forgotten to check with the neurologists, so I got it for him.'

Catherine heard his words through a fog of disbelief. The professor had always been there; no one had ever considered that something might happen to him. He had seemed immortal. 'Is it bad? I mean. . .'

'His mind is still clear.' Matt longed to touch her, if only to comfort as she worked out the implications of the professor's illness. 'That's why I agreed to continue doing his lists. Apparently previous assistants were uncomfortable with the deception, preferring to get proper acknowledgement or whatever, but it's OK by me. I get lots of surgical experience, and I happen to think the old boy is worth a little anonymous support.'

Her thoughts were tumbling and whirling like the blurred colours in a film on the wrong speed, and Catherine clasped her hands tightly to keep them from jerking in useless movement.

Matt continued to talk. 'He built up this whole department from nothing. He's forgotten more about kidney disease than I'll ever know, so as long as he can think, talk and teach I'm more than willing to do the hand work.'

Catherine finally found her voice. 'How many people know?' And how long had Matt Dunnegan had this knowledge that he'd kept to himself, even if it mattered more to some people than it did to him?

'Not many, yet. The theatre team of course, but we use the same people for all our lists. The neurology consultant who's treating him, but he's discreet.'

'How long. . .?' She couldn't finish the question.

Matt shifted in his chair and began to sort aimlessly through the papers on his desk. 'A few months. Until he has to give up, we keep going.'

'A few months?' Her world was shaking on its foundations. 'If he goes, we all go.'

'Yes,' he agreed quietly.

'But. . .the unit? What will happen to it?' And what will happen to me, to the staff, to the patients?

Matt said evenly, 'Disbanded, probably. The

academic chair will disappear and the dialysis unit will be finished.'

'But it can't be!' she gasped.

'Of course it can.' He tried to be gentle. 'It happens all the time. A vacant position is somehow never filled, the budget allocations come around, no money is assigned, and so it goes. A slow process, but inevitable. The Prof will be retired with all due honour and the search committee will find, after a suitable interval, a lack of worthy candidates.'

'That's not fair!' Catherine protested.

'Who said anything about fairness?' Matt wished she'd change the subject. There were no prizes for guessing who she was going to blame for all this. 'Besides, the current thinking is to emphasise home dialysis, not cosy little hospital units like yours.'

'It's that cosiness that makes the patients comfortable!' To hear criticism of her beloved unit was too much, on top of the devastating discovery about their department head. 'Their treatment isn't all peaches and cream, you know. Just because you work in a squeaky-clean sterile room where all the patients are unconscious and can't talk back, how can you know what our people need?'

Matt was beginning to feel very tired. That nephrectomy had been his third major operation today, and there was another to come. Plus the complaints being felt from several long disused muscles. 'What all ESRF patients need is a functioning kidney, and it's my job to find them and put 'em in. End-stage renal failure is just that—the end stage.' He rubbed his forehead and eyed her angry face. 'No matter how many frilly curtains and potted plants you stick around them, your patients are in a holding situation and nothing more.'

'They're being given life!' she protested.

'Only because, for most of them, there isn't an

available transplant. And most of them aren't well enough now to tolerate even that possibility. Including Jackie. Why was she left on peritoneal dialysis so long? Tell *me* that.'

Catherine didn't pause to think. 'Because it kept her alive. Would you rather she died? If you say yes, I don't believe it. You've changed her treatment and now, maybe, you've found a donor.'

'She should have been on haemo long before this,' said Matt. 'She was left on PD because it was convenient for everybody. Easy. Everybody was in a neat little rut. You know, Catherine,' he narrowed his eyes, 'that building is set apart from the rest of the hospital, all nicely self-contained. Very homey and comfy. Comfy can be dangerous. Just how much do *you* need that old place with the long-term patients coming in year after year for your loving care?'

'So you decide you're going to stir things up!' It seemed they'd had this argument before, but Catherine couldn't think of another answer.

Matt sighed and stretched his aching back. 'Somebody had to. If you're alive, you change. That's the nature of things.' The telephone began to ring, but he ignored it. 'If you want to keep yourself all snug and safe in that little haven, far be it for me to suggest otherwise.' He finally picked up the receiver. 'Dunnegan. . . Right, I'll be down in a minute.'

To Catherine he said, 'The next patient is prepped and waiting. Since it's one for my own list, I'd better get moving.'

She nodded, without thinking. That snug haven he dismissed with nonchalant sarcasm was her security, and now its very existence was under threat.

'See you at the Rec Club on Saturday.' Matt's hand lay lightly on her shoulder for a moment. 'Lock up when you leave, will you?'

He left, without expecting a response, and Catherine sat as if turned to stone. Inside she felt only a grey nothingness, until a dart of red appeared. Lock up? That was what he had said. She'd like to lock up Matt Dunnegan and everything he'd said or done or. . . Catherine scowled at the still flickering computer screen and turned it off with a savage twist.

If only Matt could be made to disappear as easily! The way he had talked about the dialysis patients—he really was a cold-hearted fish! Typical surgeon. Give him a knife and he'll cheerfully slice up a living body as long as it's safely asleep, but did he care what happened to living, conscious people? Homey. Comfy. He thought that was nonsense, but it was what the patients needed. It was what they all needed.

And he thought she was going to play tennis with him. Not tennis, not anything. No games at all. Not with Matt or anyone else. There were more important things to think about. Such as the imminent disappearance of an in-patient unit providing care for over fifty people. Their future was more important than any silly relationship with a here-today, gone-tomorrow visiting surgeon.

CHAPTER NINE

THE sight of Matt togged out in his immaculate whites did nothing to mollify her as she walked purposefully towards the empty tennis court. His smile was broad, but she could see the hint of relief in the easing of the furrow between those beetle brows of his.

'Can't we at least say hello?'

'Hello.' Catherine began to drag her racquet out of her case. So he had been worried she wouldn't show up, had he? Quite right too. It had been Danny's pleading that she should at least give his determined pupil a chance that had dragged a reluctant agreement from her. 'After all, he's doing all this work just for you, you know. I don't think he cares much for tennis, if you want my opinion, just wants you to get that trophy.'

Now she glanced at Danny as he hobbled on the heavy walking leg plaster and waved a strapped wrist in their direction. He called, 'Your cheering section and coach extraordinaire has arrived, Cath. Let's show them, eh?'

Catherine included him in the polite smile she directed towards their opponents, who were taking their places, before she moved off to bounce practice balls against the back of the court. She could only be grateful that the audience for this farce would be small; theirs was the first match, and, if she had anything to do with it, would also be one of the shortest on record.

The toss for serve meant she was receiving, and she pointedly ignored her partner moving up to the net.

He'd be lucky if he didn't fall over it, she thought as she began to plan their defeat in straight sets.

Matt was well aware of his partner's grudging participation, but she was here, that was all he cared about. A vaguely familiar thrill of competition was beginning to increase his heart-rate, and he altered his grip slightly. This was a game of tactics, if he could remember everything Danny had said. It didn't help if your partner was refusing to look at you, but Matt watched the movements of the other team closely. Sluggish feet on the man, and the girl's backhand was weak. He must remember that.

'Play!' The clear call brought the first serve whizzing past his ear, and Matt instinctively ducked as Catherine met it on the rise and slid it over to die at the feet of the girl. 'Love-fifteen.'

Catherine bit her lip; that had been an automatic response, and she would have to be more careful. She had better things to do than play a doubles game single-handed. She waited at the net as the next serve was directed at Matt. Moving early in expectation of an evened score, she was nearly hit in the back by the vigorous return that also surprised the server. 'Love-thirty.'

Catherine stared at Matt. He had actually made contact! A lucky fluke—it had to be. He gave her a brief nod as they changed places and his face was a picture of concentration. She realised he intended to win this game, and her heart sank. Was there nothing he admitted he could not do? Well, two had to play to win, and she had no intention of prolonging the agony.

She allowed the next serve to float by her half-hearted swing. 'Fifteen-thirty.'

Ignoring Matt, she walked casually up to the net. If he thought he could win on the offchance of occasionally making a decent return, he could think again. This time he sent the ball out of bounds. 'Thirty-all.'

Hah! Catherine began to feel more cheerful. That should teach him! Some games required skill, and a week's practice just might not be enough, especially if a man had feet the size of elephants'. She hit the next serve to make things look proper, but was disappointed when the opposing girl's backhand hit the net. 'Thirty-forty.'

Matt gritted his teeth. He didn't like people who threw games, and he had watched Catherine carefully when she and Danny had played. He knew how good she was. Stubborn woman! Thought he was an upstart, did she? Not worth the effort? With a tiny backward step he reached high for the bounce of the next serve and threw his weight behind it. Just like a long throw, and it felt good. Aimed right at the weak spot, and the opposition didn't even see it. Just like old times, and the eye was still good. 'Game, Miss Woodley and Mr Dunnegan.'

He sauntered over to the drinks stand for the break, handing a filled paper cup to Catherine. 'Surprised?' he asked.

'Just what are you trying to prove?' she hissed *sotto voce*.

'Don't like losing.'

'Sometimes you have to.'

'Not this time.'

Catherine muttered into her cup, 'They're better than we are.'

'Don't think so.' Matt was lounging comfortably, gazing around the court with a satisfied air. 'What's the matter? You chicken?'

'What. . .?'

'Afraid to win?' he jeered.

Knowing she was being baited, Catherine couldn't resist snapping, 'Winning isn't everything.'

'No?' He sounded amused. 'Cluck, cluck!'

'Shut up.' She tried to keep her voice down as she crushed her cup to a pulp.

'Cluck, cluck!' He was still glancing with apparent fascination at the ceiling as he whispered softly, 'Dare you. Double dare.'

'Time!' The umpire's call brought Catherine to her feet, and she grabbed her racquet handle with whitened knuckles.

It was her turn to serve, and she eyed the girl on the other side, hoping that backhand would improve. She directed her serve at the forehand with a ferocity that caught the girl off guard. 'Fifteen-love.'

This wouldn't do at all. Catherine glared at the broad shoulders bent near the net. Thought he knew it all, did he? Thought he could have whatever he wanted; all he had to do was lift a little finger and he would have his heart's desire. They'd see about that! She sent her serve directly to the man's forehand, and was rewarded with a clean direct return aimed straight at Matt.

She watched astonished as he rose on his toes, retreated smoothly and with what looked like a lifetime's practice sent the ball in an angled volley to land just inside the sideline. 'Thirty-love.'

He was grinning happily as they crossed the court, and he muttered in her ear, 'Much better going backwards. Especially with no tackles coming at you.'

There was nothing else she could do. He was determined, and obviously luck was on his side. Despite her best intentions it looked as if they couldn't lose. Even the opposition had sensed the resolution in the big man who seemed to be everywhere — running, jumping and chasing every ball. The sight of that hulk glowering at them across the net must be unnerving, and there was nothing Catherine could do to make him less intimidating.

She continued to play passively, accepting their winning of the second game without comment. When his turn came any hope she might have that Matt's serve would be weak or wild soon died. Danny had obviously drilled his student thoroughly in the science of aiming at the weaknesses of the opposition. It was also apparent, loath as she was to admit it, that Matt made an able student. He was a natural athlete with an intuitive eye for speed and distance of the ball, and his own balance never wavered.

The one area of play that Danny seemed to have neglected was positioning, and Catherine finally broke her silence with an angry, 'Get off my side of the court!'

He had run behind her to reach for a sliced volley she was waiting for and their racquets had collided. Even though they had satisfactorily lost the point, Catherine did not appreciate the zig-zag movements of her partner. She never knew where he was, and he seemed to be underfoot all the time.

'Decided to play, then, have you?' Matt obediently stepped back across the dividing line and smiled widely. 'Thought I had the whole place to myself.'

'This is supposed to be doubles, and you stay back there!' She pointed at the base line.

'Anything you say.' He began to jog on the spot, giving a demonstration on finely-tuned calf muscles. 'Watch that guy's curve ball. He's tried it three times already.'

'This isn't baseball.' He must think she was an idiot!

'No, it's more fun. Hah! Told you!' Matt deliberately waited as she scooped up the swerving volley and had the luck of a call that gave them the point.

She had to agree he was right about the fun. Every time Matt chased an impossible volley, a small gathering of onlookers at the sideline cheered wildly, and his answering shrugs and laughter created a spirit of camaraderie even with the two other players. They began to send the balls as far back as possible, entering into the wild spirit of play. Matt had become the star of the tournament without even knowing how to play properly!

If only he would time his approaches better she could cover her side. 'Try slowing your run in,' she told him.

With a slight raise of his eyebrows, Matt nodded. He hadn't thought of that. That must be how she reached everything with less effort. Waiting just a second longer. He'd never been very good at waiting for anything, but it was worth a try.

He watched Catherine moving in her carefully planned coverage, always ready to change direction. That was it, Matt thought. Flexibility. Something else to learn.

During the fourth game Catherine sensed a change in Matt's play. He became less spontaneous and more thoughtful, supporting her lead. Her serves were more accurate, but his were more powerful, and she was learning what to expect on his returns. Now there was absolutely no chance that they would lose, and she allowed herself to relax into effective and winning team play.

'Game, set and match to Miss Woodley and Mr Dunnegan.'

As she acknowledged the congratulations of the other players and an exuberant Danny, Catherine felt the draining away of the brief moments of pleasure. Reality was rearing its unpleasant head, and she remembered the still unresolved sense of impending loss hanging over her life. No brief athletic match play, however triumphant, could take away the feeling of emptiness left after Matt's words had seared themselves into her heart and mind. She turned away without looking at him towards the locker-room; there was nothing she had to say to him.

He watched the slumped shoulders and lowered head, now crowned with tendrils of dampened wispy curls, as she trudged away from the chattering group. There was an aura of desolation about the tall figure in the loose-fitting blue tracksuit that touched him with an unfamiliar and disconcerting feeling. Helplessness. There was nothing he could do to ease the hurt and worry his truths had brought; all he could do was follow instructions and wait.

'Do you think she'd do better if I took her home?'

'Who?' Catherine was concentrating on her needling of Mrs Murphy's arteriovenous fistula.

'Phyllis.' Keeping her eyes away from the familar procedure, the woman was looking at the plant on the windowsill. 'She might do better with some company, or maybe a bit more light. Got a good sunny place in the lounge, next to last year's Christmas poinsettia. Comin' into bloom again, it is.'

Checking the venous blood flow and adjusting the pressure dial, Catherine did not look around. 'I don't see why not, Mrs Murphy. Plant food didn't seem to help. Maybe she does need to be somewhere else.' She laid the patient's arm carefully on a pillow support before adding, 'Would *you* rather be at home? I mean, have your treatments there?'

A hint of anxiety appeared in the watery eyes. 'What do you mean, Nurse? Not come to our unit any more?'

Our unit. Catherine heard the tremor in those words, echoing her own unspoken fears. 'I was just thinking . . .about the long journey you have to get here. It might be eaiser if you had your very own machine.' She tried to keep her voice casual.

Mrs Murphy lay back on her pillows, settling in for the four hours ahead of her. 'Well now, I don't know about that. My hubby would sure take to the idea, him having to do all that driving an' all, but where we'd put it, I don't know.' She lifted her head as another thought occurred to her. 'And who would connect me up? Nobody does it like you, Nurse.'

'And I'll continue to do it, Mrs Murphy.' There were too many questions without answers, and Catherine let the subject drop. She would have to find a way of looking for the answers without saying why she needed the information. Her first attempt was with the unit sister.

'Would it be possible to give all these EPO injections at home, if the PD patients were doing their own treatments?'

Eileen Smythe continued to frown over the staff duty rota she was pencilling in for the next two weeks. 'If we had the visiting nurses to do it. I've given you half-days on Fridays, is that OK? We don't want you too tired for that tennis tournament of yours.'

The quick smile directed at her made Catherine flush. 'Yes, thank you.' Did the whole hospital know about that laughable performance? 'If the haemo patients, like Mrs Murphy, wanted a home machine, how would she get it? Or delivery of dialysis fluids?'

The older nurse glanced sideways at the younger face and answered with an air of resignation. 'I've been arguing for a year about the need for a home dialysis team. My proposal died a death with the community team committee. Budget restrictions, they said.' She pulled out a sheaf of papers from a bottom drawer. 'Take a look if you like.'

Longing to talk about the inevitable closure of their

in-patient services, Catherine merely nodded her thanks and retreated to the lecture-room with the bulky folder. At least she might learn something about financing and how to keep their patients on the best machines available.

As she was buried in the paragraphs dealing with the organisation of nursing services for home care and beginning to grasp the issues dealing with equipment supply, she had her second opportunity to look for answers. Emily came in, laden with thick texts on nephrology.

'Oh, hi. I didn't know you'd be here.'

Catherine looked up, eager to share her discoveries. 'Hi, Em. Did you ever think about doing home dialysis? It sounds really good, Sister's done this proposal. . .' Her voice trailed off as she saw her friend's face. 'What's the matter, Em? You look absolutely whacked!'

'I'm fine. Seth was up last night with a temperature, that's all.' Emily sat down with her books. 'He's all right this morning.' She smiled wearily. 'Motherhood can be a chore at times.'

Catherine looked at the clinical texts. 'Why the need for those? You don't think Seth —— '

'No, no, he's all right.' Emily shrugged. 'Josh is asking lots of questions and the public library doesn't have enough detailed stuff, so I'm doing a bit of revision.'

Catherine raised her eyebrows. 'He really *is* getting involved, isn't he? I saw some of his programs. They looked good, from what I could tell.'

'They would be,' Emily smiled. 'Nothing by halves, that's my Josh. He has to go all out, just like Matt. Must be in their diet or something.' She laughed softly. 'Josh says Matt's worse, slogging all day in the hospital, then running himself down to the bone at the Rec Club every night.'

'Well, he doesn't need to. I mean, his tennis is awful, but really, it's silly. . .'

'What's so silly about a gorgeous man working day and night to get you what you want?' asked Emily.

'But I don't want that trophy!'

Emily kept smiling. 'Well, Matt thinks you do. And he seems determined you'll get it. Nice to have someone care that much about you.' Her grin widened as Catherine tried to expostulate. 'Don't try and tell me you don't fancy him — I see that glint in your eyes, girl. And once you get caught by a Yankee, let me tell you, you stays caught!'

Her drawl reminded Catherine of another soft American accent, and she shook her head swiftly. 'There's a lot you don't know,' she said. About his attitude to caring dialysis units and his use of opportunities presented by ailing surgeons. Oh, yes, Matt Dunnegan was a first-class opportunist.

'And maybe there's a lot *you* don't know.' Her friend looked at her seriously for a moment, then shrugged. 'But be it on your own head, Catherine. Matt's a good man, and if I didn't already have the best for myself, I'd give you some competition!' Her teasing grin robbed the words of any envy, and Catherine tried to match the tone of light humour.

'He already has more than enough competition, especially anyone wielding a tennis racquet.'

Emily didn't answer, but began to flip through the detailed medical illustrations of abnormal kidneys with apparent absorption in the gruesome-looking diseases.

Realising there would be no opportunity to hint at the uncertain future of the unit, Catherine withdrew. She didn't want to talk about Matt Dunnegan, but she couldn't stop her mind from remembering. Even Mr

Petrussi became the cause of some discomfort. He was missing his second helping of pudding.

'It's because of the calcium level in your blood,' Catherine explained. 'You shouldn't be having dairy products, the apple sauce would be much better for you.'

'But Nurse, the doctor said. . .for my ulcer. . .'

This was something Catherine didn't know about. 'What ulcer, Mr Petrussi? There's no record of you having anything like that.'

'In my stomach. Over ten years, and the doctor, he said I must drink lots of milk.'

Catherine tried not to laugh; his unquestioning trust was not really funny. 'That was a long time ago, and milk doesn't help stomach ulcers anyway, it's too acidic. Is that why you've been ordering all those puddings?'

At his nod, she sighed. Faith in the infallibility of the medical profession was not always in the patient's best interests, nor the doctors', when it came to that. 'Do you think you could do without them?' she asked. 'I'm sure you'd feel much better.'

'Oh, yes, Nurse. I don't like these stodgy things. I can have fruit?'

'No peaches or grapes, and you still have to boil all those vegetables of yours.' She realised they had missed something with Mr Petrussi, never thinking to ask the simple questions. 'Please don't think me too nosy, but could you tell me what kind of house or flat you live in?'

She was still pondering the information she had gleaned, both from the patients and Eileen Smythe's written plans, when she kept her appointment at the Rec Club on Saturday. The question of how to accept Mr Petrussi's invitation to meet his family at home and not appear rude as she snooped around looking for storage space for the dozens of bags of dialysis solution he needed every week was uppermost in her mind as she nodded to the couple waiting on court.

Danny was huddled with Matt on the sidelines, their heads close in earnest conversation. She heard Danny's instructions to his pupil.

'These ones like smashing over the net, so keep your head up.'

And your feet, she thought as she approached, impatiently brushing her tracksuit leggings with her racquet.

'OK, let's go, then.' Matt stood up, gave her a brief smile and strode out on court.

Shaking her head with resignation, Catherine started to follow, but Danny reached for her sweat-shirt with his free hand. 'Give him some help, Cath. The guy's really working for it.'

'Really? What for, is what I ask myself.' Her tone was sharp, and Danny's startled blink made her briefly ashamed of herself. 'It's all right, I'll do what I can. Don't worry.'

Although she didn't really mind if they won or lost, Catherine had to admit that Matt was indeed trying, and he *had* improved over the week. One cleverly disguised drive from him wrong-footed the opponent, and her response was spontaneous.

'Well hit!'

He grinned quickly as he trotted behind her across the court. 'I've got their tactics figured out — all part of the game plan.'

She stood where she was. 'What game plan?'

'Keep them guessing.' He inclined his head towards their opponents. 'Watch this one, she slices from the forehand.'

As she obediently prepared to receive the next serve,

Catherine wanted to ask more about that game plan of his. He must know that she didn't really care about winning the silver cup, not that she hadn't wanted it, at first. . .

'Right, that's more like it.' Matt was smiling happily as her effective low return gave them the point and the first set.

'Why are you doing this?' she asked as he handed her a towel. 'You don't even like this game!'

'I must say it's beginning to grow on me.' He buried his head under a vigorously rubbed towel, and his reappearance with hair standing in multi-directional spikes made her grin. 'I never did see the point of losing, if it can be avoided. What's so funny?'

'Nothing.' Catherine rubbed her racquet handle. 'I don't want this trophy, really. . .'

'That so? Well, it's too late now. Can't stop in midstream, can we?' He had stood up and was doing a series of deep knee bends that made him look like a gigantic bouncing puppet. One with exceedingly muscular thighs, Catherine thought, as she busied herself with rearranging her shoelaces.

'I guess not,' she muttered, knowing he was not going to explain any of his actions to her. He was a law unto himself, this man, and all she could do was tag along to see what would happen.

What happened immediately was that they won this semi-final round. Catherine played a steady game and watched as Matt worked evenly with unbroken concentration. Their win was not spectacular, but the regular businesslike strokes of her partner achieved their goal. He wasn't even breathing heavily as they shook hands with the other players.

'One more. Right?'

Catherine felt a bit winded; it wasn't often that she had been left to deal with so many overheads. Danny usually took all the lobs, but Matt had left her to it. 'Yes. I think I'll be glad when this is all over.'

He looked at her sharply, but said, 'Going to stay to watch the next game?'

Looking at the door where last year's winning pair had just entered, she shook her head. 'No. The outcome is hardly in doubt, Jack and Marilyn will take it in a walk-over.'

Matt followed her glance. 'Ah, so that's the two we have to beat, is it?'

'We don't *have* to——'

She was speaking to empty air as he had loped off to get a front row seat, and Catherine gave up. He was so determined, he'd probably sit there with a notebook analysing every move. As Danny joined him, she made her way to the locker-room to change. The blue tracksuit was feeling heavy, and it occurred to her that next week she might try a slight change. It was the finals, after all.

The new tennis outfit gave her a lovely sense of freedom and, as she adjusted the embroidered T-shirt across her shoulders, Catherine admitted she also felt delightfully feminine. Short pleated skirts just hugging the hips could be quite flattering, and as she mimicked a high serve, a flick of white lace was barely visible below the hemline.

If she expected her altered appearance to elicit any reaction from Matt she was to be disappointed. Danny let out a low, appreciative whistle at the sight of his former partner dressed in formal whites, but the dark-haired man was sitting hunched over, regarding his spotless trainers with an expression of deepest gloom.

'It's not so bad. At least we got this far,' Catherine said. Obviously he had finally realised the futility of his over-ambitious plans; he must have seen Jack and Marilyn demolish their last opponents.

'Not good enough.' Matt was picking at his racquet strings as if listening to a melody no one else could hear.

She had never seen him so despondent; it seemed wrong. This was a man who never admitted defeat in anything. Something was seriously amiss, and she felt a tiny prick of fear. 'Has something. . . I mean, about Jackie, or the donor. . .?'

He looked up quickly. 'No, nothing like that. It's this,' he waved at the two now beginning their practice serves on court. 'We really don't have a chance, do we?'

Slumping beside him with a sigh of relief, Catherine said, 'It's only a tennis game. Hardly the end of the world.' She spoke lightly, hoping to raise a smile, but failed. The hospital catering chief and his secretary had moved on to the court.

Matt continued to pluck at the racquet head. 'I've got a lot riding on the outcome.'

There was an intensity in his words that made her shiver. He made it sound as if he was risking something important; somehow she hadn't thought he was a gambling man, but he might have bet a large amount of money on a win. Even that could hardly cause such a look of despair. 'You sound as if it's life or death!' she laughed.

Matt shifted his weight before standing and stretching his legs. 'Something like that.' He was looking across at the energetic pair now changing places for volley practice.

Catherine was astonished. She had been joking, but he sounded in deadly earnest. 'I don't understand. Whose——'

'I know you don't.' He ended the conversation by

striding away to join the practice. There was no more he could say. If they lost, nothing would happen the way it should. He would fail in the only thing that really mattered but there wasn't any way of explaining that. Even if he could explain, she wouldn't believe him. This time winning was the most important thing in the world, but if she didn't want them to, he couldn't do a thing about it. He couldn't win this alone.

CHAPTER TEN

CATHERINE was thoughtful as she followed him, to begin lobbing easy shots across the net. She didn't like seeing Matt so worried. It wasn't like him, not the vital, energetic and determined Matt she knew, and she wanted the old Matt back. It was the other Matt she loved, not this one. . .

She blinked at the thought and stared at the frowning angular jaw that was clenched with tension. Now was not the time for such thinking, and she readied herself for Marilyn's serve. It whizzed past her just inside the service line, and her response was too slow. 'Damn!'

Matt said nothing as they crossed. He managed to get his racquet on the next artfully placed serve but sliced it into the net.

Catherine narrowed her eyes. If Matt wanted this match so much then she was going to have to get it for him. For whatever reason, he was unhappy and afraid of losing whatever it was he thought he would lose. This time she was ready, and her backhand return flew to Jack's feet, where it stayed. Catherine smiled. Jack had put on weight since last year; that would be useful.

Unfortunately it was not Jack who was serving, and both his partner's service points were won and they had the first game.

As they sat down for the first break, Catherine could feel Matt's tension, like a coiled spring inside the lanky muscular frame.

'It's not too bad,' she said. 'First we take on that Jack.'

'Have you taken a grudge out against that poor guy?' Matt handed her a cup of water.

'He's the weaker. Sloppy footwork.'

'Isn't he going to figure that out?' Matt watched her face. 'What then?'

'Then you take him on and I get Marilyn,' Catherine answered firmly. 'She's got a wicked serve, always has had, but I think I can manage it.' She turned to him. 'You just keep the ball in play, I don't care how.'

He gave a crooked smile. 'Whatever you say, ma'am. I'll do my best.' His tone became less teasing. 'Do you think we can win?'

'You said it was important?'

'To me. Yes, it is.'

'Well then, we'll win. If you keep aiming at Jack he'll be too surprised to do anything about it.'

'That's for sure.' Matt had to agree that no one would expect him to attack with his partner's ferocity. 'What do you intend to do with the girl?'

'You just leave her to me.' Catherine stood up, throwing her towel on the chair with a defiant toss.

Matt had a brief second of pity for the female opposition, but shrugged. He had been on the receiving end of that determinedly set jaw himself, and that was one of the reasons behind the need to win today. He had a feeling that all gentlemanly rules of conduct had just gone out the window in this particular match. Catherine, when she played to win, was a formidable opponent.

That's my girl! he thought as he focused his attention on the hapless Jack, who was about to be trounced into the tarmac. If Catherine said he had to be beaten into the ground then Matt would oblige. With pleasure.

It was Catherine's serve, and she aimed each one at a different spot, varying the curve and spin with apparent randomness, keeping the others off guard.

She won her game to love; Matt had barely had to move his feet. He had certainly set something in motion, he thought, as he waited for the Marilyn serve. As expected, he failed to connect. Catherine had been right. He couldn't get near that skill.

Catherine obviously had other ideas as she sent a return from the next serve to within an inch of the baseline, sending both Jack and Marilyn back against the wall. Matt blinked. This was becoming a battle between the women, and he waited for an angry serve. Surprisingly it was off centre and he managed to return it, as instructed, to Jack, but not well enough to avoid a volley that Catherine picked up and slid across the net to drop untouched on the other side.

'Just try and hit it!' Catherine hissed as she passed Matt.

Wondering if a two-handed grip might provide better protection, Matt gamely ran forward to a short serve, but hit a wobbly lob easily put away by the expectant Marilyn.

'That's better,' Catherine nodded at him. At least he had connected, but she would have to watch for those smashes. Right, girl, now try *me* and lay off my partner. As if sensing the determination across from her, the secretary's throw faltered and Catherine disposed of the serve efficiently. The serve to Matt was also weak, and he actually sent his return to Jack with surprising speed and accuracy.

Matt shrugged as if to say, 'I'm only following orders. Sorry, buddy,' and received an answering nod from Jack. Both men knew they were being outplayed by the women.

The tie-break deciding the first set was a close thing, but won by a viciously sliced serve by Catherine.

'Enjoying yourself?' Matt asked as he lounged beside his flushed partner.

'As a matter of fact, I am.' She rubbed her arms roughly, enjoying the feel of the soft towel. Every nerve was tingling, and she couldn't remember when she had felt so alive. 'She's good, really good. Better than last year. I wonder where she got that backhand volley down-court? Nasty, that.'

Matt watched her sparkling eyes and smiled broadly. The golden glints were back in the depths of the warm hazel, and he could feel the energy flowing from every pore in that glorious skin. 'Going to win?' he asked.

'You'd better believe it!' Catherine grinned. 'You just hang on for the ride, Matt, and stay on your feet. That's all I ask.'

'I have no intention of letting go.' His words were soft and he wasn't sure she heard them. He spoke more loudly. 'About the feet, I don't know. I have some sympathy for poor old Jack. It's getting a bit warm out there.'

Catherine eyed him with some concern. 'You're not going to fall or anything, are you?' She remembered her first sight of this limping Lancelot. 'I hope you haven't had another shot of something.' That Marilyn was playing all out, and there was no stopping now.

Matt shook his head. 'Perish the thought! Lead on to the battle, my fair one. Let it not be said your sturdy squire failed at the final skirmish!'

At least he has his sense of humour back, Catherine thought as she jumped to her feet. 'Right then, squire, let's be having you on the field. The best woman is about to win.'

'That I do believe.' Matt walked behind her, managing to stop his hand just in time from brushing her shoulder.

He couldn't help his growing sense of elation as Catherine began to play to the height of her skill; he could feel the matching adrenalin flow through his own limbs. What a woman! Those long legs that seemed to go on forever were flying around the court, just as he had first seen her, grace and power in every inch of that loose-limbed body.

He did his best to keep out of her way but kept a close eye on that bouncing secretary's tendency to aim the odd slice in his direction. 'You'll need more than that to defeat my lovely,' he muttered as he sidestepped a volley that Catherine was waiting for, to send whizzing past Jack's ear. 'Just a matter of time, that's all.'

And so it proved to be. After another hour of swinging drives, stinging serves and dropped volleys — mostly from Jack — it was Catherine who emerged triumphant to reach across the net and shake her worthy opponent's hand with genuine respect. 'Thanks a lot, Marilyn. That was the best I've ever played!'

A rueful, laughing rejoinder was lost in the chatter of congratulations. Matt took the opportunity of muttering something to Jack that the women didn't hear but brought an understanding snort from the stout catering manager.

Then Matt reached out for Catherine and lifted her high above his shoulder. 'The best, the very best! And now the whole world knows it!'

Catherine squirmed in his grasp. 'Hardly the world. Don't be silly, Matt!' As she pushed against his shoulders and was forced to look down into his upraised face, it was impossible to resist his euphoric glee. He really had wanted this win, and she glowed with the knowledge she had earned that look of pure happiness, no matter what the reason. 'Put me down!'

Slowly bringing her against his chest, he slid his arms around her. 'Wonder Woman, that's who you are. Golden and glorious.' Before her feet could touch the ground he started to whirl her around in slow circling movements, humming a vaguely familiar tune.

Catherine reached around his neck for some sort of security in mid-air and felt the topsy-turvy sensations in her stomach she had tried to forget. 'That's enough, Matt! Really, you're making too much fuss.'

Reluctantly allowing her toes to finally reach solid earth, Matt kept his grip around her waist. 'You are, you know. Only a wonderful woman could have managed with such a ham-fisted klutz for a partner. Isn't that true, Jack?' he beamed over her head at their erstwhile opponents.

'Not for me to say, mate, but I'll stand the first round, then it's every man for himself.' The man waved before heading for the locker-rooms.

'We have to go,' said Catherine. The dampness of their bodies mingling was having a detrimental effect on the steadiness of her breathing. She tried to ease away from his grasp. 'There's still the presentation, you know. You'll have the cup you wanted.'

'Pity.' Matt brushed his face against her loosened hair. 'I've already got what I want.' His lips trailed across her moistened forehead. 'Salty. Nice.'

Turning her face to emphasise her point, Catherine found her mouth somehow connected with his, and the unexpected touch caused delicious electricity to start zinging up and down her spine. Breaking away with a brief laugh she took refuge in a sudden need to tidy straggling strands around her ear. 'We've got to get changed and get over to the club for the formalities, such as they are.'

Knowing she was babbling like a flustered schoolgirl, Catherine began to stuff her racquet into her holdall. 'You did want to win this thing. . .'

'I did indeed.' Matt watched her, an enigmatic smile

tugging at his mouth. He began to tidy his own belongings. 'Just how long does this affair go on?'

'Most of the afternoon.' She started off the court and found him loping easily beside her. 'There's a lunch and speeches. . .just the usual. And you don't come in here! This is the ladies'!'

'I always wanted to know what goes on in there.' Matt looked as if he was seriously considering entering the forbidden territory before he grinned at her unbelieving stare. 'I will await your reappearance impatiently. And speaking of appearances, just how formal is this do?'

Catherine answered, 'Nothing much really,' before making her escape through the locker-room door. Behind it she leaned against the coolness of the gleaming tiled wall and took a deep breath.

This final match had been a revelation. For the first time she had wanted to win something, but not for herself. For the giant man who had tried so hard to learn something new. And probably thoroughly disliked, she thought to herself. Seeing him dejected and disheartened had been painful, and her insides still shrivelled at the picture of his shoulders bent in defeat before they had even started. Regardless of his reasons, she couldn't let him suffer without at least putting up a good fight.

His smile at their victory had made it all worthwhile, but she had to admit that she shared his obvious joy in triumph. She had played better than she had ever imagined was possible, and all to get Matt Dunnegan his silly trophy cup. He brings out the best in me, she thought, as she headed for the showers. What was that tune he had been humming in her ear? Something about being long and tall and no changes being made on the Wabash Cannonball. She giggled happily as the sharp spray massaged her limbs in rhythm with the foolish lyrics, and danced a careful watery jig while sloshing scented lather through her hair.

Luckily the room was empty as she came out to towel herself dry. Catherine cleared a circle in the steamed mirror and grinned at the shining face reflected on the glistening surface. This was a special day, a day for letting her hair down. Hurrying into clean underclothes, she scrunched her hair dry before reaching for her short woollen dress. The clinging softness against her scrubbed skin was warm and sensuous, matching the inner glow growing steadily at the thought of Matt's touch.

'He's the most exciting man you've ever met,' she addressed the image now marred with rivulets of water while adjusting the brown Alice band that allowed the golden earrings to twirl in clear view, the luminous pearls cradled in their nests of gilded stems. 'And very, very special.'

As she grabbed her stuffed sports-bag, she remembered Emily's comment about having someone care for you, enough to get you what he thinks you want. And that's just what I did, Em. Got him what *he* wanted, and I do care. I certainly do care.

'Well! Just how long does it take. . .?' Matt's words of complaint died on his lips as he stared at her emerging from the locker-room.

Catherine stopped, disconcerted by the frown creasing those black brows. 'What's the matter?' She angled awkwardly to check her short hemline. 'Is anything showing?'

Those damned earrings had appeared again. Matt cleared his throat before answering blandly, 'Nope. Just fine all around. I like your hair.' He reached for her coat and held it for her. 'Guess I'm not dressed exactly for anything grand.'

She smiled at the familiar patterned sweater worn

over rich maroon corduroy trousers. At least he wasn't wearing trainers, but the casual shoes matched the open-necked shirt collar. 'Ties aren't expected,' she told him.

'That's a mercy. I suppose I could always use shoelaces.'

His subdued tone was unexpected, and Catherine wondered if he was uncomfortable at the prospect of attending a ceremony he obviously hadn't expected. However, his quiet demeanour lasted only until they entered the Rec Club, where long tables were groaning under the buffet food prepared by the bustling Carlos. Their arrival was greeted with cries of 'At long last!' 'Now we can eat' and 'Who's got the trophies?'

'Here they are. All shined.' Carlos held up the tiny silver cups. 'How do you like the streamers, eh, Catherine?'

Looking up at the silvery garlands swaying precariously from the ceiling lights, Catherine smiled. 'A bit early, Carlos, but they're very pretty.' Giant paper snowflakes were jostling with strands of red and green linking fluttering hexagonal bells, all changing colours in the slowly rotating strobe lights. Even the bulky jukebox was festooned with a seasonal drapery of scarlet tissue and emerald ribbons. The overall effect was a cross between a winter grotto and a circus fairground.

Matt seemed to absorb the light-hearted ambience with delight, accepting the joking comments of his audience as he received the silver trophy that looked like a Lilliputian trinket in his large hands. He rose with a grandiose gesture for silence.

'To my partner. . .' he bowed deeply to Catherine now seated before a heaped plate of cold meats and salads '. . .and to the worthy opposition.' Jack and Marilyn bowed graciously to loud applause. 'This is an unexpected victory, and I would like to thank my coach. . .' he grinned at Danny '. . .and my teacher in the third grade, not to mention my great-great-grand-mother. . .' His cheerful imitation of long-winded speeches ended in loud boos and catcalls, during which Matt readily took the hint to sit down. He whispered in Catherine's ear, 'Most of all, I owe everything to my partner.'

'Too true.' She was concentrating on the generous lunch, fortunately free of Carlos's chilli peppers.

He glanced at the rapidly disappearing mound on her plate. 'Good girl! You've got the appetite of a truck driver, but God knows where you put it all.' He was toying with his own portion.

'What's the matter?' She waved a fork at his plate. 'It's good.' She couldn't think of anything that would put this man off his food.

'I'm too keyed up.' Matt was looking around. 'What happens now?'

'We eat and we go home.' Catherine speared a last cucumber slice. Out of the corner of her eye she could see his leg beating a silent tattoo against the chair leg. He did seem to be wound up. 'You can relax now. You've got what you wanted.'

'Mmm.' He was still gazing around the room and called out, 'Carlos, does that bubble machine work?'

'Sure, Doctor. My beauty can still sing a tune. Wait, I'll show you.' The stocky Spaniard patted the curved top, hit a button, directed a soft kick at the side and nodded happily as the scratchy melody of an old rock-'n'-roll song burst above the general hubbub. Loud groans and rude comments greeted the unexpected sound, but Jack leapt up, grabbed Marilyn's hand and began a creditable version of a hip-twisting dance step. He was soon joined by others, and Matt began the rhythmic clapping in support of their efforts.

'That's better. We need a little activity.' Now he was tapping his feet cheerfully and grinned at Catherine. 'Want to try?'

'Forget it.' She watched the gyrating couples. 'I prefer to keep my lunch right where it is, thank you.'

'Spoilsport!' He rose to cross over to the machine, threading his way through the dancers and stood in serious consultation with Carlos before punching a button. He returned to tower over Catherine, holding out his hand. 'This one will be for you.'

As the new selection clicked loudly into place, the others stood expectantly, and a general murmur of disapproval echoed Catherine's reaction, 'Carlos seems to favour the old-time favourites.'

Matt stood his ground. 'Don't knock the oldies but goodies. Some things don't change. Come on.'

'Oh, all right.' As the sweetly lyrical voice of the well-known singer trilled from the old jukebox, she allowed him to guide her to the edge of the slowly circling dancers. Now there were a few quiet sighs of nostalgic recognition as Catherine said, 'Our grand-fathers must have listened to her while they dodged artillery shells.'

Matt chuckled as he drew her close. 'The war's over now, my lovely.'

Allowing herself to curve against the solid shoulder so close to her ear, she had to agree. She was feeling very peaceful indeed; the music spoke of yearning and longing to be home, away from turmoil and uncertainty. Just where she was now. Without speaking, they moved in swaying arcs beneath the sparkling snow-flakes that rustled with the gently circling dancers. She felt as if she could float through the air and touch the soundless snowbells drifting above her head. If Matt could lift her higher. . .just a little bit further. . .

The singer's voice faded into silence, but Catherine

was reluctant to come back to earth. She stayed curled in the circle of his arms, breathing in the faint musky aroma that was becoming as familiar as her own heartbeat.

'Got to go.' It was Jack's voice coming from somewhere in the distance, and she turned her head to shut out the unimportant sound. 'We'll have another go next year and give the girls a run for their money, eh, Matt?'

Next year. Catherine felt an odd lump in her throat. There wouldn't be a next year, at least not with Matt. She slowly withdrew her cheek from its warm resting place. The music and the song had ended.

Matt tightened his arm briefly as he felt her slide away. Damn. He supposed he couldn't keep her this close indefinitely, not that he wasn't going to try. 'See you, Jack. Time we got on with the chores, my lovely. The stores will soon be shut.'

'What do you mean?' Catherine felt distinctly grumpy. She had been lost in a lovely fantasy and was in no mood for unpleasant realities. Did he always have to be so practical?

'Saturday shopping. We'd better get a move on.' He had moved away to gather up their bags, tipping both winners' trophies into his case. 'I need strong arms to help carry the stuff.'

'I don't want to go shopping. . .'

'Hurry up. Do you know where they sell zucchini?' He had slung both bags over his shoulder and was waving farewells.

Trying to shake the haunting strains of the music out of her head, Catherine felt only confusion. As he pulled at her arm, she made a grab for her coat before she found herself being hit by the brisk wind outside the door. 'What's zucchini?' she queried.

'Long, green, curved and crunchy.' Matt took her

arm and was marching along the footpath. 'And very tasty.'

It would have to be food, she thought. He had assumed she was willing to participate in his domestic chores, and she was disinclined to argue. Besides, he had taken her silver cup as well as his own; to get it back she would just have to follow him.

Their trail led through a variety of food shops, and Catherine waited patiently with the shopping trolleys while Matt discussed, argued and debated the merits of every purchase with shopkeepers who all appeared to know him well. She discovered zucchini meant courgettes, yams were sweet potatoes and pumpkin did not come in tins.

Finally he seemed satisfied, and as he handed her a bulging carrier bag, she said, 'What, no pickled onions?'

'You're right! I forgot them. Bless you!' With a quick kiss on her astonished mouth, he shot back to the vegetable market stall and returned with a large jar. 'Where would I be without you?'

'Carrying your own shopping.'

He grinned at her scowling face. 'It's not far now. And I've got the pumpkin, after all.'

Feeling as if her arms might drop off at any minute, Catherine trudged after him, noting with a grudging gratitude that at least he had slowed down a bit. In the deepening November twilight he looked like a hulking Stone Age hunter laden down with bags and pouches filled with provisions for a lengthy winter. And here comes the humble subservient mate lagging behind, she thought darkly. Trying to flex her aching fingers, she glanced enviously at uncurtained windows they passed where warm lights indicated that the inhabitants were safely taking their ease by welcoming hearths.

It was the time of evening when the human eye could

see most clearly. Objects assumed a crystalline clarity
in the small islands of light they passed, and Catherine
became fascinated by the hidden glimpses of moving
figures captured at an instant in their lives—stencilled
silhouettes watched by an unseen audience for a frozen
moment, before the watcher moved on to be left
wondering. What happened next? Did that lifted
teacup move up or down? Maybe it crashed to the
floor. Or, better still, maybe it got hurled across the
room in the general direction of a pigheaded, overbearing male. . .

'Here we are.' Matt had finally stopped walking.

Catherine muttered under her breath as she staggered down an ill-lit set of stone steps. She remembered Emily's description of a grotty basement flat.
Her curiosity was piqued; now she might learn a little
bit more about this man.

The sudden flash of light as he turned on the inside
switch startled her, and she tripped over the step.

'Here, watch yourself!' Matt angled an elbow in her
direction; it was his only free joint unimpeded by heavy
bags or unwieldy vegetables. 'The landlady put in such
weak bulbs I couldn't see anything, had to jack up the
wattage.' He waited until she regained her balance.
'Food in the kitchen, and I'll be with you in a minute.
Make yourself at home.'

Dumping her burdens inside the door where he
indicated, Catherine rubbed her arms vigorously to
restore the depleted circulation while she took a look
around. Home? There wasn't much homelike about
this place so far as she could see.

The hallway was long and narrow, obviously the full
length of the old Victorian house, and the lounge
opposite the open arch of the kitchen was barely
furnished with one couch, two faded upholstered arm-
chairs, a low metal coffee-table and a table with folded

leaves shoved against one wall. There were two non-descript prints on the walls, but nothing to indicate the personality of the person who occupied the room.

As she moved further down the hall, Catherine wondered if this was what minimalist décor meant. It couldn't be much more minimal than this. She peeped around a door that was obviously a bedroom and noted the crisp bright green duvet. At least something was new, even if the unknown landlady had provided the one sign of comfort. Noises of activity from the kitchen gave her the confidence to venture in for a closer look.

A wooden bureau with a chipped top held only a man-size box of tissues and a plastic box — once used to package fifty-cc syringes, she noted — holding a motley arrangement of pins, buttons and a small rectangular velvet box. There were no photographs, no personal mementoes, nothing to give away private idiosyncrasies.

She headed further down the hall, peeping into the open bathroom, nodding at the expected shining sterility of the tiles. He could probably do surgery on that floor, she thought. There was an institutional look about the uncluttered surfaces. This was a man who left few traces of himself, Catherine thought, as she turned to look at the end of the hallway. He must like to move around the world without encumbrance.

There was a bolted door at the end of the house, and she stood, irresolute for a moment, before tugging at the rusted handle.

'Leaving so soon?' The grating sound brought Matt to the kitchen arch.

'Where does this go?' Catherine asked, pulling at the heavy door. As it opened a crack, the smell of damp earth drifted past her. 'Are there steps? Oh, you've got a garden!' Leaving the door open for some light, she gingerly decended the three steps into the shadowed space. She could just smell a faint sweet aroma filtering through the gloom.

From the little she could see, the walled space was filled with a riot of overgrown plants crowding over old flagstone pathways. It was another world, hidden from the outside, and all sounds seemed distant and muted. As she brushed aside clinging leaves the sweet smell grew stronger. Just as she thought she had found the source of the perfume, she was left in sudden and total darkness.

It was Matt, blocking the light from inside, and for an instant, Catherine was reminded of the first time she had seen him — overshadowing the Professor that first day. This time he was a figure in black surrounded by the orange glow from the hall. 'You're blocking the light. I can't see.'

He stepped aside, and in the shaft of illumination she saw it — a single rosebud struggling for life, sending faint hints of its delicate fragrance in this unseen garden.

'Look, it's perfect.' Catherine gently touched the tip of the narrow stem. 'A winter rose, alone in this jungle!'

'I see.' Matt came to stand where she was bending in the foliage. He reached out to follow her hand.

'No!' Catherine put her hand on his arm.' Let it grow in peace. It might still flower.'

His arms crept around her. 'I wouldn't dream of harming such beauty.' His breath was warm against her ear. 'Cold? Come inside.'

Catherine nodded. The lovely tingling in her limbs had begun again as the smell of musk mingled with the scent of the rose. It was right to leave this enchanted garden to its secrets. The tiny pink bud would open of its own accord.

CHAPTER ELEVEN

THE light and heat of the sitting-room were welcoming, and Catherine exclaimed, 'What's all this?'

'A small collation, my love.' Matt guided her to the settee and reached for the wine bottle lying in crushed ice. 'A private celebration.'

She watched as he deftly removed the cork. The sparkling wine had not been one of the purchases during their recent perambulations around the local supermarkets; he had prepared this in advance. She accepted a glass with a crooked smile. Had he really been as unsure of winning as she had thought?

Matt raised his glass. 'Not champagne, I'm afraid, but a subtle little drink without pretensions, I'm sure you'll agree. Here's to us.'

She took a sip and waited while he settled himself on the floor, leaning close to her knee. These surroundings told her nothing about him; a more direct approach was needed. The wine might mellow him. She said, 'Why did you want to win so much?'

'I told you—I don't like losing.' He took another taste of wine. 'Mm, not bad.' He looked up at her. 'And you did the winning.'

He had turned the topic back to herself. 'I'll bet you didn't win all the time as a. . .whatever. . .football player?'

'Quarterback. And I did, most of the time.' Matt propped himself up with an elbow across the edge of the settee. 'All that took was practice. And knowing the rules.'

His head was close to her leg, and Catherine touched

the single strand falling across his temple. The combination of the wine and his nearness was creating a lovely feeling of comfortable muzziness. She said thoughtfully, 'That's why Josh admires you so much. You won everything. He said. . .well, he told me what you've done.'

Matt jerked his head abruptly, turning to look at her face, his hand paused in mid-air as he had been about to put down his glass. 'What did he say?'

The sharpness in his glance was puzzling. 'About the car and the promotion. He says he owes it all to you.' Why did he look so serious?

Taking a deep swallow of wine, Matt answered evenly, 'He did that himself. He's a good salesman, and the equipment is great.'

Knowing she had missed something important, Catherine remained silent, as Matt gradually returned to his relaxed position. She noticed he had placed the two tiny silver trophies on the coffee table next to the wine. At least now he would have at least one personal item in this room. 'Do you like living here?'

'Hm?' He looked up, surprised at the question. He smiled into the hazel eyes watching him so closely; at this moment there was nowhere else he would rather be. 'It suits me fine.'

'But there aren't any. . .well, nothing looks comfortable——'

His deep chuckle interrupted her. 'You mean no frills and furbelows?' His hand reached up to enclose hers. 'I have everything right here that any man could ever want.'

The delicious tingling was started again, this time up her arm, and soon it would start the delicate patter around her heart. She tried to concentrate, despite the depth of meaning she read clearly in those grey eyes fastened on her face. 'I mean, you don't even have any pictures, of your family, or anything. . .'

Matt eased himself up higher, keeping her hand firmly clasped. 'I don't need reminders of the woman I love.' He grinned at the tightening of the fingers curled in his palm. 'My mother's face is as clear before me as yours, my lovely. Except she has brown eyes, not glinty gold specks like yours. Beautiful specks.' He stretched up to examine her closely, and Catherine could only take a deep breath. His mouth was so close, so tantalisingly near. . .

'I much prefer those little dots. . .ah, there they go again!' Matt seemed entranced by her eyes and Catherine blinked several times, making him draw away with a quick laugh. 'Are you asking about my family, my love? Is that what you want to know?'

'Well, yes, I guess. . .' It was as good a subject as any while she tried to sort out what was happening and what she was going to do about it.

'All right. A quick résumé. Mother lives with two sisters in Boston. Widowed and worked for years as a nurse, would you believe?' He grinned at Catherine's surprise. 'Oh, yes, my love, I know all about shifts and overtime and never enough time to do everything.' He leaned back against her knee and placed his empty glass neatly beside the silver cups.

'I heard that all my time growing up. She was earning our upkeep, and that's why the football lark — I had to earn the college fees. Medical education is long and expensive, but as long as the knees lasted I was OK. I was probably the oldest player in the College Bowl!'

'And that's when Josh met you.' Catherine allowed her free hand to trace a light path across the back of his neck.

Matt nodded, leaning his head back against her

touch. 'He used his brains to get through; I had the brawn. Same purpose.'

Catherine murmured softly, 'You had a lot in common, even toy trains.' She smiled at the memory of two grown men's delight in a surprise birthday present.

The dark head under her hand stilled. 'That was different.' He pulled himself forward, leaning his elbows against upraised knees, keeping his face away from her. 'It was my brother who had the train set. I hadn't seen one for nearly twenty years, but that little shiny locomotive brought it all back.'

'You have a brother.' For some reason she had not expected this, thinking she would have sensed if he had siblings after all.

'Had.' The word was soft. 'He was my twin, and—well, he was ill. He needed a transplant and he didn't get it. He. . .we were ten years old. Just Jackie's age.'

Catherine felt a physical jolt deep within her. Understanding was flooding her mind—about Jackie, about his determination, his solitude, and even the unstoppable energy, as if to make up for the one who was missing. 'He died.' she queried gently.

'Yes,' Matt answered quietly. 'He had liver disease, and there weren't any liver transplants in those days, at least not where we lived.' He waved his hand aimlessly in the air. 'So there went half of me. Just gone. I decided someone ought to try and do something about that.' He turned and met her gaze, with a crooked smile. 'Every time I see a child swollen up with fluid, I remember, and that's when I decide *I'm* going to be the winner, not the disease.'

Overwhelmed by the need to let him know how well she did understand, Catherine wrapped her arms around his neck, burrowing against his cheek. 'I'm so sorry, Matt. I hope you always do—win, I mean.'

'I hope so too.' Matt reached up to cup her chin softly and pulled her down beside him. Their lips met in a lingering kiss of gentleness and sorrow, deepening into an intensity of wanting that defied explanation.

As his fingers touched the sharp edge of the golden earrings, Matt deepened his pressure, before murmuring huskily, 'These are beautiful, my love, but may I take them off?'

She nodded in the hollow of his throat, feeling his lips graze her ear-lobes as the weights were gently removed. His fingers were tracing a line of electric sensation down her neck, searching for the tiny throb beating in rhythm with the quickening dance of her heartbeat. There was a faint trail of moisture on her cheek, and she cradled his head against her softness. 'Shhh, it's all right, Matt. I understand,' she crooned in whispers. 'You're not alone. I know, I know.'

He gave a strangled sound as he buried his face deeper and his arms tightened convulsively. Catherine lowered her head to touch her lips to a glistening teardrop. His loss had become hers; he did not have to suffer it alone any more.

'Oh, my God, Catherine!' Matt pulled her across his lap and his mouth covered hers, hungrily searching for the missing part of himself.

She felt no sense of surprise at the rush of desire coursing through her body at his touch; whatever he wanted or needed from her was his and only his. There were no more questions.

His fingers were at the neck of her dress, and in a swift movement his hand moved to gently circle her surging roundness.

'My love. . .' He breathed deeply as he slowly drank in the ivory whiteness with his eyes before touching his lips to the swollen pink tip waiting for him.

'Yes, Matt, yes. . .!' Twining her fingers around his

neck, Catherine allowed herself to float in a flood of desire and curled against his hardness. She felt an unwelcome coolness as he withdrew his lips.

He was making every attempt to control his breathing as he whispered against her ear, 'You do bring out the deeper part of me, my love.' He nuzzled against the sweet-smelling mass of auburn hair flowing over his arm. 'I think we should——'

'Should what?' Catherine reached up to plant tiny kisses along the angular jaw. What was this funny, wonderful man thinking about now? Did he never stop thinking?

Matt tipped her chin up to see his face. 'Make sure we both know the rules.' He brushed a thumb along the pert nose with that delightful dusting of freckles. 'This isn't a game.' He smiled into her half-lidded eyes lit with the golden glow he loved. 'It might be wiser to walk off the court before starting this kind of match play.'

Catherine slid her hands down the corded muscles of his back. She had watched the movement of every sinew and tendon for weeks; now she wanted to touch him and feel each ripple under her fingertips. She murmured, 'I thought you wanted to win.'

'Oh, I did, I did.' His smile widened. 'And what I wanted to win was you. I didn't give a hoot about the tennis game.'

'You didn't?' She backed away a little, but not very far.

He shook his head, watching her reaction. 'And I play for keeps, my love.' He slid a glance at the discarded earrings but immediately looked back at her face. 'Those are the rules.'

Whatever he wanted was fine with her. Catherine cocked her head and looked at him sideways. 'What would have happened if we'd lost?' she asked.

Matt scowled; now she was teasing. 'I guess that would have been what you wanted.'

'Precisely.' Pleased with having made her point, Catherine reached up to wrap her arms around his neck. 'I won it, Matt. Me. But I did it for you. You looked so miserable and it mattered so much, I just had to.' She kissed the bump on his nose. 'Does that answer your question, whatever it is?'

Matt wasn't exactly sure what he had been asking, and that golden light in her eyes was blinding his thoughts. He enfolded her in his arms and with one powerful swoop gathered her up from the floor. 'I don't know, my love,' he breathed against the glowing cheek laid against his shoulder. 'Maybe it's wrong to question your dreams.'

Clinging tightly, Catherine pressed closer to the strength lifting her high into the air. She smiled against the freshly shaven jaw, murmuring, 'Just don't trip over your feet, partner, or we'll both go down to defeat.'

'Not a chance, my love.' Matt's deep chuckle was husky. 'The fruits of victory are ours.' He held his warm burden with infinite tenderness, carrying her swiftly with purposeful strides. 'They must be savoured. . .' he laid her down and bent to caress her parted lips '. . .slowly. . .and fully. . .to the very last. . .'

The intoxicating sweetness of her engulfed him and there was no more time for words.

It was a low throbbing that woke Catherine, and she squinted at the tumbled mass of bright green over her head. A faint aroma of musk brought back the memories, and she snuggled back into the rumpled duvet. Never again would she leave this haven of love; she would just wait until he came back and they would continue the magical matching that gave every cell in her body the glorious sense of being newly alive. She wiggled her bare toes over the edge of the bed. Every nerve wanted to dance with joy, and she stretched each languorous limb, luxuriating in the sensation of complete satiation. Miracle Matt, indeed!

Another, more immediate rumbling claimed her attention. Not all of her was wholly satisfied; it seemed her stomach was demanding attention. Catherine frowned. It was a nuisance that eating was a necessity, requiring a return to the world outside this precious cocoon, but she groaned softly and half sat up, blinking against the morning light.

Light? Wondering what time it was, she reached for an oversized terrycloth robe laid across the foot of the bed. There was no sign of her clothing, and she padded sleepily in the direction of the bathroom. Appetising smells were drifting down from the kitchen; obviously Matt was back at his favourite activity. Well, hopefully his second favourite activity! She grinned at the thought as she noted the new heart-shaped bar of pink soap and fluffy yellow towels awaiting her. He had thought of everything she could want.

She scrubbed quickly; the tantalising smells of bacon and fresh coffee were impossible to resist. A peep into the wicker laundry basket in the corner revealed only emptiness; that loud noise must have been a washing machine. Tightening the cord of the robe around her waist, Catherine headed for the kitchen. It was definitely time to say good morning to the busy bee in the midst of his morning chores.

Matt's smile was as bright as the day when she poked her head around the kitchen arch. 'Am I allowed in?' she queried.

'Good morning to you.' He raised his hands in mock

dismay. 'I'd enfold you in my manly embrace, but you'd get smothered in sage and onions.'

Catherine beamed at the sight of him, stripped to the waist with a striped apron wrapped around his pyjama bottoms. 'I love sage and onions.' She moved to wrap her arms around his torso and nuzzled against his chest.

'That's taking unfair advantage.' He let out a mock groan, dropping a kiss on her damp head. 'If you carry on like that we'll both starve, as the chef will be rendered powerless!'

'I don't believe it.' Catherine kissed the edge of his chin and giggled as he backed away. 'Cowardy custard!'

Matt grinned down at her. 'Would you kindly concentrate your interest on breakfast?' He bent to plant a feathery kiss on her upturned nose, then waved a hand towards the counter, splattering bread crumbs on her shoulder. 'I need the bacon dripping for this creation.'

Reluctantly turning her attention away from him, she began to munch the crispy slices, perched on a stool to watch. 'Is that lunch?' She glanced at the fat fowl awaiting what must be several pounds of stuffing.

He nodded as he reached for the empty frying pan. 'Tom Turkey here is doing us the honour of being the main course. In case you didn't know,' he turned to look at her, his smile deepening, 'today is Thanksgiving, and I, for one, have a great deal to be thankful for.'

Catherine could only nod in agreement; his smile was warming every inch of her, and she felt she must be flushing bright pink. 'How can you give it a name? That's like eating a friend!'

'Not at all.' He turned back to his task, spooning the savoury filling into the prepared bird. 'Our Native Americans knew how to love everything that gave them life.' He noticed her looking around and indicated a crusty loaf. 'Toaster's on the shelf above the washer.'

Catherine looked at the pile of fresh laundry; she could see her tracksuit in the midst of it. She reached for the loaf and cut a thick slice. 'Am I supposed to name the bread?' she asked.

'Wouldn't do any harm.' He began to sew with an elegantly curved needle. 'The Indians took good care not to offend the spirits of what they needed to survive, and if the grain or game disappeared, everybody perished, so all the spirits had names.'

'They must have spent a lot of time doing that.' Catherine watched the flashing needle; only an expert surgeon could stitch up a turkey that fast.

'All their lives.' Matt gave the finished bird a final pat. 'And that's why we give thanks, with the help of friend Tom here.'

Unaccountably reminded of her patients' dependence on their machines, and Mrs Murphy's predilection for naming things, Catherine asked, 'Isn't he a bit large?'

'Not for five. Well, four and a bit.'

'What?' she queried.

'Josh and Emily are coming. I promised Josh candied yams, but nowhere could I find black-eyed peas.' Matt was beginning to pile his bowls into the sink. 'And I've still got the pumpkin pie to do.'

'What time?' Catherine asked, glancing at the kitchen clock. What if they found her here like this?

He grinned at her. 'Any time now. I'm sure Josh will appreciate your fetching appearance as much as I do.'

'And what about you?' she shot back. 'Emily will be most impressed.'

'I doubt it. I think she likes what she's got,' he answered, dragging out the soon-to-be-demolished pumpkin. 'Besides, I bet it takes me less time to get all gussied up than it does you.'

Smothering a retort, Catherine decided discretion was the better part of valour and retreated, after fishing out her clean underclothes from the pile of fresh laundry. She found her dress hanging in the bedroom wardrobe, just as if it belonged there, she thought, dressing hurriedly. She hoped her friends would refrain from comment at seeing her here, with every evidence of having spent the night. Explanation would not be easy.

In the event, she needn't have worried. Their guests arrived just as Matt had discarded his impromptu cooking attire for a clean shirt and jeans and was withdrawing a golden-crusted pie from the oven.

'Hey, it smells like home!' Josh headed straight for the source of the tempting aromas, leaving Catherine to help Emily carry in the excited toddler.

'Hi—having the car makes these trips so much easier. No, Seth, leave those alone.' Emily grabbed at her son's hand as he reached for one of Catherine's dangling earrings. 'I really like those. They're the ones from Mark, aren't they?'

'Yes——'

'No.' Matt had heard his own name and answered in unison with Catherine. For a moment, he stared at her, puzzled, above the child's head. He could have sworn Emily had said his name, but Catherine was just looking at him curiously. No matter. Her attention was being demanded by a hungry little boy and in the clamour of voices he could have misheard. He asked, 'Anyone for a pre-prandial libation?'

'If that means a drink, I wouldn't say no.' Josh had returned with a cheerful smile. 'After all, it's not every day we have a family Thanksgiving, is it?' He met his wife's eyes and they looked at each other in a moment of silent understanding before Emily laughed and bounced Seth on her lap. 'Someone I know would like a cup of something. Do you have any apple juice, Matt?'

That secret message between her friends had held a depth of meaning, Catherine knew, but it had shut out all others. It wasn't until Josh was patting his stomach with satisfaction that she was to learn what it meant.

'Mighty fine food, Matt. Just like down home.' He reached across to hold his wife's hand. 'I think this is the right time, sweetie.'

Emily nodded, held his hand against her cheek for a moment and smiled her agreement.

Josh turned to look at Matt, now lounging on a chair opposite Catherine curled up in a corner of the settee. 'We've had enough time for talking, Matt. We've decided to go for it—all the way.'

Matt said nothing, and Catherine felt the hairs on the back of her neck prickle with apprehension. There was something about Josh's tone of voice. He was still talking.

'The way I see it, you've thrown me a long one.' He grinned like a schoolboy. 'My big dream, that was. The great Matt Dunnegan, throwing to me for the big score. I'd sprint like the wind and win the game, and be a hero, like you.'

Matt was not smiling. 'This is no game, Josh.'

'Yeah, I know. But it's still the big one.' Josh was still holding Emily's hand. 'And we're agreed. It's not often a boy from Baton Rouge is offered a chance to really be somebody, not like this.'

'You are somebody, Josh. You don't need to prove anything.' Matt spoke quietly.

'I know that. Maybe I'm not saying it right.' Josh frowned to himself, and Catherine watched him closely. She wanted to ask what was going on, but there was tension in the air and she knew she was being excluded.

Matt was looking from Emily to Josh and back again. 'You know what's involved — Emily must have told you. It might not even work.'

'But you think it will.' This came from Emily.

'All the signs are excellent.' Matt was talking seriously from one professional to another. 'Everything matches that needs to. Yes, I do think it will work, but it's not for me to decide.'

Josh had straightened up. 'No, it isn't, Matt. It's for me, for us, to decide. And we have. We go for it.' He nodded firmly. 'You said she's in good shape — well, so am I.'

Catherine found her voice. She had added up two and two and didn't like the answer. 'She? Is she Jackie?' she asked.

'Yeah.' Josh looked at her, with a proud smile. 'She's a great kid, isn't she? And I'm a match for her. Me, would you believe it?'

Almost choking on the words, Catherine said, '*You*? You're Mr N. Saint?'

CHAPTER TWELVE

MATT spoke before Josh could answer. 'We found out by accident, using our own samples for data testing, and he has the right T and B cell match.' He saw the look on her face and turned to the others. 'I'll start setting things up. I'm getting a perfusion machine from the blessed Mrs Blessington, and that will help things considerably. Emily can explain to you, Josh. Some time in the next couple of weeks; I'll give you several days' notice. Will your employer give you the time off, Josh?'

'Just let them try and stop me! Nobody's going to stop Josh Beatty from going the distance this time!'

'I wish you'd give up on that game stuff,' said Matt smiling, 'but if you insist on it, then I'll do my damnedest to throw you a straight one.'

'We know that,' Emily answered. 'Now, I think we'd better get on home. Our son and heir is ready for his own bed, I think.'

In the midst of the bustle of their departure, Catherine acted like an automaton, trying to take in what had been said. How could this happen? How could Matt even think of such a thing? She spoke warmly and casually to her friends, hugging them both, but her mind was swirling with questions and all the answers came back to one person. This was all Matt Dunnegan's doing.

'So, let's have it.' He was waiting for her as the door closed. For some reason he had known she would disapprove, and he couldn't have discussed it earlier without Josh's permission anyway. He would have to

172

be prepared for negative reactions, and this one was sure to be a jim-dandy.

'I don't understand.' Catherine sat down, staring unseeingly at the faded carpet. 'I mean, how. . .?'

Matt answered evenly, 'Theoretically, there's a match for everybody somewhere in the world. If we had a universal tissue-typing bank like the bone marrow people, we might find matches pretty far-flung all over the globe. Who knows?'

'But he can't be a genetic match!'

'It's only the specific cell antigens we need most to avoid rejection, not the whole DNA bit.' He kept his eyes on her reaction. 'There's been a lot of travel around the world over the centuries, and we'll all end up with similar genotypes eventually, with occasional mutations, if you look at it that way.'

'But *Josh*! How can you use *him*?' she cried.

'Use?' he queried.

'What if Seth needed something? Josh isn't even related to Jackie. How can he be a living donor?' She had never heard of such a thing happening before.

Matt kept his voice even. 'There's no rule about it. Most of the time it's assumed that parents or a sibling will donate to a family member; strangers aren't even asked. Only leukaemics are considered in that light.'

'They can grow more bone marrow. Josh can't grow another kidney once you've used him!'

'Again with that word!' Matt sighed. 'I am not using him, as you put it. He's an adult and does have a say in the matter.'

Catherine felt her anger growing. 'He thinks you're the greatest thing since. . .well, the invention of the wheel, and he'd do anything you suggest! The great Miracle Matt Dunnegan!'

'Oh?' His voice held a dangerous calm.

'Just like everybody else around here.' Now she felt

the unstoppable rush of words pouring out. 'Take Geraldine, and Danny. I saw that notebook where you've got everybody's passwords. Anything to get the information you wanted. Even Sister thinks the sun rises and sets at your command. And poor Danny, you used him to get that silly thing.' She gave the twin silver cups on the coffee-table a disparaging snort.

Matt remained silent, his face inscrutable.

'And don't tell me you're not using the professor! You even said so yourself—you get to do all the renal surgery without any possible objection from him. What do you think he might feel about that? Do you ever consider how other people might feel about your charging around on your white horse, leading whatever crusade you've created for yourself?' She paused for breath.

'Keep going,' he drawled. 'You might as well get it all off your chest.'

She shot the most painful bolt. 'I suppose I was a crusade as well?' she glared at him, but he remained silent. This was not exactly the desired response. 'Was that why you decided to take up tennis when you hardly knew which side of the racquet was right side up? Was it? Why don't you say something?'

He shifted his weight from one hip to the other as if making himself more comfortable on the narrow chair. 'You want me to say no? You think I was so keen to learn a sport where I had to bob around, dressed in white shorts, playing giant hopscotch? Why would I give up precious time away from hunting down elusive donors for sick people?' He leaned forward, continuing to speak very slowly.

'Of course I was willing to make an idiot of myself. I wanted to be near you, and you were so prickly it seemed the only way. It was obvious that no one expected surgeons to visit the dialysis unit regularly, despite the deterioration of several patients who might benefit from some surgical intervention.'

The tiny thrill of knowing he had worked for her was buried in the message of his final words. Deterioration. That was what he really thought. 'Well, you won, didn't you?' she demanded. 'You got what you wanted. Even me!'

'That's hitting below the belt, Catherine,' Matt said quietly.

'A most appropriate phrase,' she answered repressively. 'You just have to win everything, don't you? Well, not this time, Matt Dunnegan. I'm not going to be another trophy, like this thing!' Standing up abruptly, she inadvertently swept one cup off the table, but left it where it was. 'Where's my bag?'

He rose at the same time, waited until she finished her tirade and turned to the kitchen. 'I'll get it. Your things are still in the laundry pile.'

As she grabbed at the open bag and stuffed the tracksuit through the opening, she growled, 'Thank you. You'd make somebody a simply marvellous wife!'

'Something like that.' His words were so soft she barely heard them as she moved towards the hallway.

'You don't need to see me out,' she said stiffly.

'Sit down. I'll get you a cab. Sit!'

The unexpectedness of his raised voice brought her to a halt. 'I'm surprised you didn't hire the old Duchess.'

As he finished speaking rapidly into the telephone, Matt responded in a tired voice, 'I had other plans for that distinguished lady, not quite suitable under the present circumstances.'

'And what does that mean?' she demanded.

'Let it go, Catherine. Whatever I say is probably going to be misinterpreted.' He held out her coat.

Shrugging herself into the cold jacket, Catherine

moved to avoid the weight of his hands on her shoulders. It wasn't fair what his touch could do to her. The sooner she left this monk-like flat, the better she would feel.

The taxi ride passed in a blur. The cabbie asked for no payment; again Matt had thought of everything. He had always been strides ahead of her, planning secretively for all of them, including her closest friends. Unnecessary surgery on a healthy person — it beggared belief!

Slumping down on her narrow bed, she caught sight of a dog-eared postcard lying on the floor. It was another colourful picture from Mexico and brought forth the tears waiting to surface underneath the anger.

'Hang up the holly and put the kettle on. Arriving shortly. Love, Mark.'

At least there was one person she could depend on, someone who didn't trick or use people to gain his own ends. But somehow the knowledge that Mark would soon be here did not provide the expected sense of relief, and Catherine crushed the card in her fist curled under a pillow soon wet with tears.

Surveying the debris of his Thanksgiving table, Matt stood motionless before bending to pick up the rejected silver cup. He held it for a long moment before walking slowly into the kitchen, saying to the empty walls, 'It seems some victories can be short-lived, however sweet.'

With great care he placed the trophy beside its companion in the dark recesses of a cupboard, shutting the door before turning to begin clearing away all signs of recent celebration. There was no time now for looking back. Perhaps, after a little girl received an extra-special Christmas present, maybe then there might be time for other wishes to come true. With the luck they would all need, anything could happen.

Scrubbing vigorously at an encrusted baking pan, Matt concentrated on the problems looming in the immediate future. He frowned into the lemon-scented soapsuds. Where was he going to get access to electron micrography in this neck of the woods? A live donor transplant was not exactly your run-of-the-mill operation. A bit dodgy, as an auburn-haired beauty might say. He grinned at the thought. 'Just you wait, my lovely! One miracle at a time. The game isn't over yet.'

As soon as she saw the name on the theatre list, Catherine felt her shoulders tighten just as if she were the one who would have to spend hours bent over the operating table. She tried to shake off the feeling and vaguely heard someone speaking behind her. 'Sorry?'

'I said, Happy birthday, Catherine.' Eileen Smythe was holding out a steaming mug of tea. 'You must hate having a birthday so close to Christmas, missing all the extra presents children expect.'

'How did you know?' Accepting the cup, she tried to smile. 'About my birthday, I mean?' Her feeling of something being missing had nothing to do with childish gifts.

'I've been checking our staff records and noticed it.' The unit sister beckoned her into the office. 'Can I have a word, please? It's about that proposal you read. It's up before the hospital board again.'

'That's good.' Catherine tried to focus her mind on the plans for home dialysis, but she was only reminded of the limited future of the unit. Everything seemed to be coming to an end.

'This time I think they'll have no choice.' Eileen sat down and motioned to a chair beside her. 'Now tell me about your home visits.'

As she described the possibilities for storing Mr Petrussi's dialysis fluids in a kitchen cupboard and the boxroom Mrs Murphy could use for her machine, Catherine kept her mind away from the intrusive thought that at this very minute Josh Beatty was having a kidney removed.

At the end of her report Eileen said, 'Well done, Catherine! We'll be able to see all of them settled at home, I think. How do you feel about keeping up those visits?'

'What do you mean?' queried Catherine.

'If we have to disband as an in-patient unit there's no reason why we can't continue as a community-based team — if the board accepts our proposal.' Eileen gave Catherine a quiet smile. 'I saw that Levodopa prescription too, you know, and I have lunch regularly with the theatre sister. We think Prof will announce his resignation after Christmas, and that will give us about six months to reorganise.'

A genuine sense of relief swept through Catherine as the weight of carrying secret knowledge evaporated. 'You knew all the time?' she exclaimed.

'For about a year. That's why I prepared plans and why I think we can develop a home dialysis team. What do you think?'

'Of course we can!' Catherine answered excitedly. 'If we could get some help from a training team ——'

'I've already contacted the college.' Eileen shuffled a few papers on her desk. 'I've got the schedule of refresher courses somewhere here — ah, here it is. We could get everybody in before the spring. Do you think you could be available in, say, two months? Nothing special planned?'

There was a knowing twinkle in the older nurse's eyes that Catherine chose to ignore. 'What about Emily? Does she know?'

'Not yet. She needs time to see her husband recover before thinking about changes here. It's not easy coping with change, especially when it all seems to happen at once.'

Catherine nodded agreement; that was an understatement. She seemed to be in a maelstrom of fluctuating feelings and thoughts. She hadn't seen Emily since that unusual Thanksgiving Day and her spontaneous outburst. She was glad that her friends wouldn't know of her reaction to their decision, which had lasted only long enough to leave a sense of anger about being taken by surprise. Some people never gave any warnings about what they were planning, that was the trouble.

As she continued her ward duties, Catherine kept an eye on the clock, and during the afternoon she began to feel the unconscious tension ease. It was over. For better or worse, it had been done. Now there was only Jackie to think about. Nothing else was important.

In that thought she was wrong. It was Eileen Smythe who came to find her flushing out tubing in the utility-room. 'Catherine, can you get over to ITU, please? There's an emergency dialysis——'

'Not. . .?' Barely able to get the word past the sudden constriction in her throat, Catherine was already pulling off her work gloves.

'Yes, I'm afraid so. It's Josh Beatty, and Emily has asked for you.'

Already moving out the door, Catherine said, 'I'm on my way. Only Mrs Murphy has still to be weighed. Can you——?'

'Yes. Let me know what's happening.' The unit sister was waiting with Catherine's coat and slung it over her outstretched arm.

Her brain in a whirl of fear, Catherine sped out of the unit, conscious of nothing but the deafening pounding of blood in her head. She was breathless as she slowed down before the charge nurse in the intensive therapy unit. 'Mr Beatty?'

He pointed to a curtained cubicle near the desk, and she paused to steady herself. There could be no shaking hands now; Josh needed the best she could provide.

Behind the curtain Emily was seated beside the bed holding her husband's hand, a pile of red wool lying discarded in her lap. There was a dialysis machine as well as an opened tray of surgical instruments waiting. Beside the tray Matt Dunnegan was drawing on surgical gloves.

He did not look up, but Catherine could see the tightness in his back and shoulder muscles beneath the flimsy theatre shirt. She began to scrub at the bedside sink and looked around for a pair of gloves.

Emily caught the movement from the corner of her eye and a wan smile of gratitude crossed her face. 'I'll get them, Catherine.'

At the sound of her name Matt's hands paused for an instant, but he did not turn his head as he picked up a gleaming cannula. 'I'm going to put a tube in your thigh, Josh. A bit of local anaesthetic and you won't feel a thing.'

'OK, Matt. Whatever you say.' Josh's voice was weak and drowsy, but he tried to smile. 'A bit of a fumble, eh?'

'No way. Just a slight case of pass interference, and we'll deal with it.' Matt waited for Catherine to finish gowning without looking at her. 'Sometimes one kidney objects to taking over the total load of work at such short notice, so we'll give it a bit of a rest.'

Taking her place beside him, Catherine heard the casual tone of reassurance, but knew he was far from feeling as calm as he sounded. She held out an antiseptic swab on a forcep above the already shaved area and at his nod began to clean the insertion site above the femoral vein. It was the fastest mode of entry used as a temporary access for emergency dialysis. Emily would know this, and had almost certainly explained to her husband. With luck, this would be a one-off dialysis. With luck.

A quick glance from Matt startled her, and Catherine flushed. She must have spoken aloud again. 'You're in luck, Josh.' She tried to cover her carelessness with a quick smile. 'Now you've got the best of St Damien's renal team at your beck and call!' As she said the words, she realised they were true. Matt *was* the best, in every way, but he was unlikely to be thinking this at the moment. The slim needle had been slid in during her chatter.

'That's right, love.' Emily picked up Catherine's tone. 'It won't be long before you'll feel better. As soon as those whirring things start, everything will be all right.' Her husband merely winked at her sleepily before he drifted back into a post-anaesthetic oblivion.

The procedure was completed smoothly, and Catherine immediately began the dialysis as Matt made a silent exit. Knowing there was nothing more she could do for her friends while they waited for the treatment to correct the short-term renal failure, she made her way to the staff-room. There was one thing she could predict about Matt — when in need of solitude or peace he would inevitably head for the nearest kitchen.

He was slumped on a plastic-covered couch and looked up briefly as she came in. 'You don't have to say it,' he muttered.

'Say what?' She eased herself down on the corner of the couch. He had that air of defeat that sat so incongruously on his broad shoulders and moved her so deeply.

'I told you so.' He sighed. 'If I hadn't interfered, none of this would have happened.'

'You were right. I was wrong.' Catherine looked at him steadily. The red-rimmed circles around his eyes told her he had spent as many sleepless nights lately as she had.

'Right?' He lifted his head to frown at her. 'About what? Leaving a healthy patient with one kidney that's currently malfunctioning?'

'You said yourself post-op renal failure is expected. It's not your fault, and he is healthy. The kidney will compensate, you know that.'

Matt dragged his hands over his face with a heavy gesture. 'Right now, I don't know anything.'

Catherine couldn't allow him to lose faith in himself. He was the man who set the world to rights, who charged in to do battle for the weak, who filled her world with life and love. . .'Josh will be fine, I just know it. And Jackie too. We'll be —' She stopped.

'We'll be what?' Matt was leaning with his head back, watching her through heavy-lidded eyes.

Catherine rushed her words. 'And we'll be fine too. Really.'

With a gentle smile, Matt took her hand in his and tucked it under his arm, held fast against his chest. 'Ah, my love! It's no wonder you rant and rail at me. Guess I need it when I get too filled with my own ideas of what needs doing. What would I do without you to fight for the poor people I like to push around to fit my picture of what the world should be?'

Catherine inched closer to that slumped shoulder. 'Sometimes the world needs a little pushing.'

Matt slid an arm around her shoulder and gave her a quizzical smile. 'At the moment I'm too tired to push anything, or anyone, anywhere.'

'Good,' Catherine murmured happily as she snuggled against him, feeling the glow of his relaxation spreading to her own limbs. This might be a good time to think about other changes. 'Did you know we're going to be a home dialysis team at the unit? Sister says we can do it more cheaply than in-patient care, and when Prof retires——'

'Oh, Sister says, does she?' Matt grinned against the soft sheen brushing his chin. 'Good old Smitty! I always thought she was a step ahead of the rest of us.'

'And the patients will still need surgery.' She angled her head upwards to see his reaction. 'You could always stay here and do all the nephrectomies and transplants, and maybe urology and——'

His laugh interrupted her. 'I could, could I?' He tipped up her chin to examine the flushed face shining with eagerness. 'There might be a few conditions attached to that possibility. You remember the rules?'

Wishing he would stop talking and just kiss her, Catherine said, 'Remind me.'

'For keeps, my love. And that means——'

His words remained unsaid as a heavy shuffle of feet caught his attention and he looked across at an unknown man standing in the doorway. Hiding his irritation at the untimely intrusion, he put on a polite expression. 'Can I help you?' he asked.

'Oh, I'm awfully sorry. Didn't mean to interrupt, but they said Catherine was in here——'

At the first sound of the man's voice, Catherine had leapt out of Matt's arms with a glad cry of welcome. 'Mark!'

There was something vaguely familiar about the slim young man hugging Catherine with such enthusiasm, but Matt was too busy struggling with his own anger to think about it. The person with the name so like his own was treating Catherine with an altogether too intense a degree of possessiveness. Matt decided enough was enough, and rose to approach the interloper. 'How do you do? I'm Matt Dunnegan.'

'Oh, yes, I know who you are. You're the one who's stolen my Catherine's heart. Have to be, from what I saw going on, eh?' The young man began to rummage in his bulky pockets. 'I've got something here, for both of you, if I can just find it. Got it!'

As Catherine accepted the object wrapped clumsily in cloth Matt took a closer look at the visitor. He was tall, with sun-darkened skin and wearing what could most charitably be described as a well-worn bush jacket. There was something likeable about him as he beamed happily at them both, and there was something definitely familiar about his eyes.

'Look, Matt! Look at what he's brought!'

Squinting at the misshapen blob that resembled a lumpy person carved from some dark wood, Matt remarked drily, 'Looks like it could use an abdominal paracentesis, if you ask me.' He was grateful that at least it wasn't another pair of delicate earrings.

'Don't be silly! It's a. . .well. . .' Catherine began to blush, and as if having second thoughts, hid the figure in one of her uniform pockets. 'Never mind.'

'I say, I hope I haven't come at a bad time. I mean, from what Catherine said, I thought it was all arranged,' Mark put in anxiously.

Catherine tried to explain, seeing the familiar furrow of black brows. 'I write to him, you see, and sometimes he thinks—well. . .'

'Yes, that's it. I read what she doesn't say, if you get my meaning.' The tanned face was beginning to look embarrassed. 'I thought you were getting married and rushed to get here in time. I didn't want to miss it, after all.'

Matt was rapidly losing patience. 'You what? Who

are you? Other than the provider of gifts? You gave her those earrings, didn't you?'

'Of course. And today's the birthday, so I had to get here, didn't I?'

'Whose?' Feeling in definite need of rescue, Matt turned to Catherine. 'Yours?'

'Ours!' With a wide smile, she reached for the young man's hand. 'Mark is my brother. I'm sorry, I thought I'd told you. I did try to say how I understood when you told me. . .' She raised her free hand to brush his face softly. 'Mark is my twin and he knows everything I think and feel sometimes even before I know it myself.'

'Twin?' Now he could see it—the same hazel eyes, the same shock of thick auburn hair, lightened by a tropical sun. He'd bet on Mexican sunlight. The mist of confusion was rapidly dissipating.

'Sorry if I've done something wrong.' The young man was shifting his feet uneasily.

Matt had found himself on firm ground. Very firm ground. 'Not at all. Glad to meet you, Mark. You came just in time—for the wedding. I'll need a best man, and you're elected.'

'Oh, I say, that's great! Love to. . . Matt.' The bronzed face beamed with pleasure.

'Wedding? What are you talking about?' Catherine's voice struggled to make an impact in the rush of congratulations between the two men. 'I didn't say——'

Matt turned to her. 'Too bad—we've decided. Now *where*, is the question.' He looked back at his soon-to-be brother. 'I've got the rings and the transport. Great old Duchess!'

'What duchess?' demanded Mark. 'Are we moving in exalted circles, then? Can she get to Switzerland?

At last report, the parents were there, and they wouldn't want to be left out ——'

'That's enough!' Catherine was nearly shouting. 'Go away, Mark. There isn't any duchess, at least not a real one.' She began to push her brother out of the room. 'It's too difficult to explain. I love you dearly, but just this once, Mark, go away!'

'Switzerland is good.' Matt just had time to answer before the laughing brother was bundled out of the door and he was faced with those golden glints again. He sighed happily at the familiar and deeply loved sight. His Catherine was about to let fly again. 'So, when can we go?'

'We can't go anywhere and you know it! There's too much work to do here ——' Her protests were stopped in mid-flow by a sound and thorough kiss. She struggled for air, finally surfacing with a slight gasp. 'Now, stop that! You know as well as I do, Matt Dunnegan, that there's too much to do.'

'I don't know anything of the sort.' He kept his arms around her while he began kissing each of the singularly beautiful freckles across that pert little nose. 'We'll need time to get my mother across the ocean. She's always fancied mountains, but will find the Alps pale in comparison with the Appalachians. Never mind.' He began to travel across her glowing cheek. 'She'll love you and will start feeding up that skinny brother of yours.' A deep chuckle sounded in her ear. 'A twin, yet! Knows you better than you do yourself, eh?'

Rapidly losing all hold on reality, Catherine made another attempt. 'Not always. Sometimes he takes too much for granted, like some other people.' The delicious pitter-pat dance around her ribcage was growing in intensity. 'Really, Matt, we can't just run off. . .'

'I didn't say that. I intend to drive off with you and that brother of yours until we find a chalet hidden at the tip-top of the highest mountain, and then——' he deepened his whisper against her neck ' — and then, my love, we will have our own very private thanksgiving. Properly.'

'Haven't you forgotten something?' Her murmur was barely audible.

'What?' Matt lifted his head. 'I love you, I've got the rings, the transport, and now both families are accounted for. We'll get young Jackie sorted out by Christmas and then we'll be off. Just thee and me. What else?'

She smiled against his chest. 'What about me?'

'But you're everything! You're the reason for all this. What do you mean?' He sounded genuinely perplexed, and Catherine couldn't smother her giggles.

'You haven't asked me anything,' she told him.

There was a moment of silence before Matt spoke. 'Ah, did I forget to ask you to marry me? Well, sorry, but I know you love me.' His arms tightened around her. 'And that's what people do, isn't it? For keeps, I said. Those are the rules. I thought you knew that.' He pulled back a fraction to try and see her face. 'You *did* know that?'

Suspecting that with this determined, single-minded man these words were the best she was going to get, Catherine smiled into the deep grey eyes. Was there just a hint of pleading there? He might not be the most romantic man she had ever known, but he was certainly the best loved. 'Yes, Matt, I knew.'

'Then that's all right, then.' He returned to thorough exploration of each hidden angle of silken skin under her ear-lobes. 'You know, my love, I might even learn to live with frilly curtains.' He paused thoughtfully. 'But not in the kitchen, though. I draw the line at that!'

Catherine allowed herself to drift into the dance of joy filling her being, reaching up to trace a question mark with her fingertips across his temple. 'And the garden, that needs clearing——'

Matt drew back with a startled grunt. 'What *is* that?'

Before she could answer, she felt his hand reaching into her pocket and pulling out the wooden carving. It must have dug into him, and she said, with a teasing smile, 'Even Mark doesn't know how prophetic that can be!'

Taking the figure from his hand, she held it up sideways so that the distended abdomen was clearly visible and watched his eyes widen in understanding.

'Is that what I think it is? No ascites?'

Catherine's eyes twinkled. 'No, it's a fertility symbol. Little did he know just what it might mean!'

Matt let out an exaggerated groan. 'Twins! Heaven help us, there'll be no escape.'

As their eyes met in mutual laughter and love, they both spoke at the same time, sending their united understanding clearly down the outside corridor. 'Matched doubles!'

The explosion of sound was brief and was followed by a profound silence more suited to the environs where survival was a battle and life a victory well worth the winning.

ESCAPE INTO ANOTHER WORLD...

...With Temptation Dreamscape Romances

Two worlds collide in 3 very special Temptation titles, guaranteed to sweep you to the very edge of reality.

The timeless mysteries of reincarnation, telepathy and earthbound spirits clash with the modern lives and passions of ordinary men and women.

Available November 1993   Price £5.55

MILLS & BOON

LOVE ON CALL
4 FREE BOOKS AND 2 FREE GIFTS
F R O M   M I L L S   &   B O O N

Capture all the drama and emotion of a hectic medical world when you accept 4 Love on Call romances PLUS a cuddly teddy bear and a mystery gift - absolutely FREE and without obligation. And, if you choose, go on to enjoy 4 exciting Love on Call romances every month for only £1.80 each! Be sure to return the coupon below today to: Mills & Boon Reader Service, FREEPOST, PO Box 236, Croydon, Surrey CR9 9EL.

— — — — — — — — — | **NO STAMP REQUIRED** | — — — — — — — —

YES! Please rush me 4 FREE Love on Call books and 2 FREE gifts! Please also reserve me a Reader Service subscription, which means I can look forward to receiving 4 brand new Love on Call books for only £7.20 every month, postage and packing FREE. If I choose not to subscribe, I shall write to you within 10 days and still keep my FREE books and gifts. I may cancel or suspend my subscription at any time. I am over 18 years. Please write in BLOCK CAPITALS.

Ms/Mrs/Miss/Mr _____ **EP63D**

Address _____

_____

Postcode _____ Signature _____

mps
MAILING
PREFERENCE
SERVICE

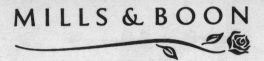

MILLS & BOON

LOVE <small>ON</small> CALL

The books for enjoyment this month are:

SWEET DECEIVER Jenny Ashe
VETS IN OPPOSITION Mary Bowring
CROSSMATCHED Elizabeth Fulton
OUTBACK DOCTOR Elisabeth Scott

♥   ♥   ♥   ♥   ♥

Treats in store!

Watch next month for the following absorbing stories:

SECOND THOUGHTS Caroline Anderson
CHRISTMAS IS FOREVER Margaret O'Neill
CURE FOR HEARTACHE Patricia Robertson
CELEBRITY VET Carol Wood